Melanie Milburne

THE MARCOLINI BLACKMAIL MARRIAGE

D0039238

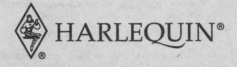

TORONTO • NEW YORK • LONDON
AMSTERDAM • PARIS • SYDNEY • HAMBURG
STOCKHOLM • ATHENS • TOKYO • MILAN • MADRID
PRAGUE • WARSAW • BUDAPEST • AUCKLAND

Recycling programs
for this product may
not exist in your area.

ISBN-13: 978-0-373-12845-7

THE MARCOLINI BLACKMAIL MARRIAGE

First North American Publication 2009.

Copyright © 2009 by Melanie Milburne.

All about the author...
Melanie Milburne

MELANIE MILBURNE read her first Harlequin novel when she was seventeen and has never looked back. She decided she would settle for nothing less than a tall, dark and handsome hero as her future husband. Well, she's not only still reading romance, but is writing it, as well! And the tall, dark and handsome hero? She fell in love with him on the second date and was secretly engaged to him within six weeks.

Two sons later, they arrived in Hobart, Tasmania—the jewel in the Australian crown. Once their boys were safely in school, Melanie went back to university and received her bachelor's and then her master's degrees.

As part of her final assessment, she conducted a tutorial on the romance genre. As she was reading a paragraph from the novel of a prominent Harlequin author, the door suddenly burst open. The husband she thought was working was actually standing there dressed in a tuxedo, his dark brown eyes centered on her startled blue ones. He strode purposefully across the room, hauled Melanie into his arms and kissed her deeply and passionately before setting her back down and leaving without a single word. The lecturer gave Melanie a high distinction and her fellow students gave her jealous glares! And so her pilgrimage into romance writing was set!

Melanie also enjoys long-distance running and is a nationally ranked masters swimmer in Australia. She learned to swim as an adult, so for anyone out there who thinks they can't do something—you can! Her motto is "Don't say I can't; say I Can Try."

To Pauline Samson, for all the work she does for swimming in Tasmania and nationally. She has sat on various pool decks, tirelessly timing both mine and other people's swims for the National Aerobic Trophy. Winning it in 2007 was a great achievement for such a small but dedicated club, but really all the credit must go to Pauline, for there is only one thing worse than swimming eight hundred meters of butterfly, and that is sitting there timing it!

"None that three months living with me as my wife will not rectify," he said, his eyes boring into hers with steely intent.

Claire stared at him, her heart doing a pretty fair imitation of her car's recalcitrant engine on a cold morning. "You're blackmailing me to come back to you?" she choked out.

"The word *blackmail* implies a lack of choice," he said with an enigmatic tilt of his lips that was close to a smile. "In this instance I am giving you a choice, Claire. You either return to our marriage for the duration of my stay in Sydney or I will press property-damages charges against your brother. What is it to be?"

Magnificent & Merciless

Two red-hot Italian brothers, as different
as night and day but united by the
Italian fire that burns through them....

They are magnificent.

They are merciless.

They are the Marcolini Men!

There's fire in their blood, passion in
their veins...love in their hearts?

CHAPTER ONE

IT WAS the very last thing Claire was expecting. She stared at the lawyer for several seconds, her brain whirling, her heart suddenly beating too fast and too hard. 'What do you mean, he wouldn't agree to it?' she said.

The lawyer gave her a grim look. 'Your husband flatly refused to sign or even to accept the papers for a divorce,' she said. 'He was absolutely adamant. He insists on a meeting with you first.'

Claire gnawed at her lip for a moment. She had hoped to avoid all contact with Antonio Marcolini during his lecture tour of Sydney. It wasn't supposed to happen this way. Five years had passed; a divorce after such a long separation was surely just a matter of a bit of paperwork? Leaving it in the lawyer's hands was meant to make it easier for her to move on.

She *had* to move on.

'Unless you have specific reasons not to meet with him, I suggest you get it over with—and soon,' Angela Reed advised. 'It may well be he wants to end things on a more personal note, rather than formally through the legal system. Ultimately he will not be able to prevent a divorce, of course, but he could make things drag on—which would incur even more legal fees for you.'

Claire felt a familiar twist of panic deep inside at the thought of more bills to pay. She was sailing far too close to the wind as it was; a long drawn-out legal process would just about sink her. But why on earth would Antonio want to see her after all this time? The circumstances under which their relationship had ended were hardly conducive to a friendly cup of coffee and a chat about old times.

She took a deep breath and met the lawyer's speculative gaze. 'I guess one face to face meeting won't hurt,' she said, with a sinking feeling deep in the pit of her stomach.

'Think of it as closure,' Angela said, as she pushed back her chair and rose to her feet, signalling the consultation was at an end.

Closure, Claire thought wryly as she made her way out to the street a short time later. That was why she had activated the divorce proceedings in the first place. It was well and truly time to put the past behind her. She owed it to herself to embrace life once more.

The phone was ringing as she unlocked the door of her flat and, dropping her bag and keys on the lumpy sofa, she picked up the receiver. 'Hello?'

'Claire.'

Claire gripped the phone in her suddenly damp hand, trying to suppress the groundswell of emotion that assailed her as soon as she heard the smooth, even tones of Antonio's accented voice. Oh, God, if this was how she was going to be just listening to him, how on earth was she going to cope with seeing him? Tiny beads of perspiration broke out on her upper lip; her heart was hammering and her breathing becoming shallow and uneven.

'Claire.' He repeated her name, the velvet stroke of his deep tone making every pore of her skin lift beneath the layers of her winter-weight clothes, and the blood to kick start in her veins.

She swallowed tightly and, closing her eyes, released his name on a stuttering breath. 'Antonio…I was…er… just about to call you…'

'I take it you have spoken with your lawyer?' he asked.

'Yes, but—'

'Then you will know I will not take no for an answer,' he said, as if she hadn't spoken. 'No meeting, no divorce.'

Claire felt her back come up at his arrogance. 'You think you can order me about like some sort of puppet?' she asked. 'Well, damn you, Antonio. I am not—'

'Face to face, Claire,' he said, in the same indomitable tone. 'I believe there is no better way to do business.'

Claire felt tiny footsteps of ice-cold fear tiptoe up her spine at his words. 'I—I thought you were here for a lecture tour, not to socialise with your soon to be ex-wife,' she said, trying for a cool and unaffected tone but failing miserably.

She glanced to where she had left the newspaper announcing his arrival, lying open, even though every time she walked past, it drove a stake through her heart to see his handsome features smiling as if everything was right with his world.

'It is true I am spending the next three months in Australia, lecturing and operating for the charity I began in Italy,' he said.

It had not been the first time Claire had read about his charity, called FACE—Facial and Cranial Endowment—which raised millions of dollars for the surgical reconstruction of patients with severe facial injuries. She had followed the progress of some of the cases he had operated on via his website, marvelling at the miracles he performed for his patients. But then miracles only seemed to happen to other people, Claire reminded herself bitterly. Her brief marriage to Antonio had taught her that if nothing else.

'But I must say I find it rather strange you did not expect me to want to see you in person,' he continued.

'I find it inappropriate, given the circumstances,' she returned a little coldly. 'We have nothing to say to each other. I think we said it all the last time we were together.'

And how, Claire thought as she recalled the bitter words she had thrown at him. Angry, bitter words that had done nothing to ease the pain of her loss and the final barbarous sting of his betrayal. He had been so cold, so distant, and clinically detached in that doctor way of his, making her feel as if she had no self-control, no maturity and precious little dignity.

'I beg to differ, Claire,' he countered. 'The last time we were together you did the speaking, and all the accusing and name-calling, if I recall. This time I would like to be the one who does the talking.'

Claire's already white-knuckled fingers tightened around the phone, her heart skipping in her chest. 'Look, we've been separated for five—'

'I know how long we have been separated,' he interrupted yet again. 'Or estranged, as I understand is the more correct term, since there has been no formal division of assets between us. That is one of the reasons I am here now in Australia.'

Claire felt her stomach tilt. 'I thought you were here to promote your charity…you know…to raise its profile globally.'

'That is true, but I do not intend to spend the full three months lecturing,' he said. 'I plan to have a holiday while I am here, and of course to spend some time with you.'

'Why?' The word came out clipped with the sharp scissors of suspicion.

'We are still legally married, Claire.'

Claire clenched her teeth. 'So let me guess.' She let the words drip off her tongue, each one heavily laced with scorn. 'Your latest mistress didn't want to travel all this way so you are looking for a three-month fill-in. Forget it, Antonio. I'm not available.'

'Are you currently seeing anyone?' he asked.

Claire bristled at the question. How he could even *think* she would be able to move on from the death of their child as he had so easily done was truly astonishing. 'Why do you want to know?' she asked.

'I would not like to be cutting in on anyone else's territory,' he said. 'Although there are ways to deal with such obstacles, of course.'

'Yes, well, we all know how that hasn't stopped you in the past,' she clipped back. 'I seem to recall hearing about your affair with a married woman a couple of years back.'

'She was not my mistress, Claire,' he said. 'The press always makes a big deal out of anything Mario and I do. You know that. I warned you about it when we first met.'

To give him credit, Claire had to agree Antonio had

done his very best to try and prepare her for the exposure she would receive as one of the Marcolini brothers' love interests. Antonio and Mario, as the sons of high-profile Italian businessman Salvatore Marcolini, could not escape the attention of the media. Every woman they looked at was photographed, every restaurant they dined at was rated, and every move they made was followed with not just one telephoto lens, but hundreds.

Claire had found it both intrusive and terrifying. She was a country girl, born and bred. She was not used to any attention, let alone the world's media. She had grown up in a quiet country town in Outback New South Wales. There had been no glitz and glamour about her and her younger brothers' lives in the drought-stricken bush, nor did Claire's life now, as a hairdresser in a small inner-city suburb, attract the sort of attention Antonio had been used to dealing with since he was a small child.

That was just one of the essential differences that had driven the wedge between them: she was not of his ilk, and his parents had made that more than clear from the first moment he had brought her home to meet them. People with their sort of wealth did not consider a twenty-three-year-old Australian hairdresser on a working holiday marriage material for their brilliantly talented son.

'I am staying at the Hammond Tower Hotel.' Antonio's voice broke through her thoughts. 'In the penthouse suite.'

'Of course,' Claire muttered cynically.

'You surely did not expect me to purchase a house for the short time I will be here, did you, Claire?' he asked, after another short but tense pause.

'No, of course not,' she answered, wishing she hadn't been so transparent in her bitterness towards him. 'It's just a penthouse is a bit over the top for someone who heads a charity—or so I would have thought.'

'The charity is doing very well without me having to resort to sleeping on a park bench,' he said. 'But of course that is probably where you would like to see me, is it not?'

'I don't wish to see you at all,' Claire responded tightly.

'I am not going to give you a choice,' he said. 'We have things to discuss and I would like to do so in private— your place or mine. It makes no difference to me.'

It made the world of difference to Claire. She didn't want Antonio's presence in her small but tidy flat. It was hard enough living with the memories of his touch, his kisses, and the fiery heat of his lovemaking which, in spite of the passing of the years, had never seemed to lessen. Her body was responding to him even now, just by listening to his voice. How much worse would it be seeing him face to face, breathing in the same air as him, perhaps even touching him?

'I mean it, Claire,' he said with steely emphasis. 'I can be at your place in ten or fifteen minutes, or you can meet me here. You choose.'

Claire pressed her lips together as she considered her options. Here would be too private, too intimate, but then meeting him at his hotel would be so public. What if the press were lurking about? A quick snapshot of them together could cause the sort of speculation she had thankfully avoided over the last five years.

In the end she decided her private domain was not ready to accept the disturbing presence of her estranged husband. She didn't want to look at her rumpled sofa a few days hence and think of his long, strong thighs stretched out there, and nor did she want to drink from a coffee cup his lips had rested against.

'I'll come to you,' she said, on an expelled breath of resignation.

'I will wait for you in the Piano Bar,' he said. 'Would you like me to send a car for you?'

Claire had almost forgotten the wealth Antonio took for granted. No simple little fuel-efficient hire car for him—oh, no—he would have the latest Italian sports car, or a limousine complete with uniformed chauffeur.

The thought of a sleek limousine pulling up to collect her was almost laughable, given the state of her own current vehicle. She had to cajole it into starting each morning, and go through the same routine at the end of the day. It limped along, as she did, battered and bruised by what life had dished up, but somehow doggedly determined to complete the journey.

'No,' she said, with a last remnant of pride. 'I will make my own way there.'

'Fine. I will keep an eye out for you,' he said. 'Shall we say in an hour?'

Claire put the phone down after mumbling a reply, her heart contracting in pain at the thought of seeing Antonio again. Her stomach began to flutter inside with razor-winged nerves, her palms already damp in apprehension over what he had already said to her, let alone what else he had in store.

If he didn't want a divorce, what did he want? Their marriage had died, along with the reason it had occurred in the first place.

A giant wave of grief washed over her as she thought about their tiny daughter. She would have just completed her first term in kindergarten by now—would have been five years old and no doubt as cute as a button, with her father's dark brown eyes and a crown of shiny hair, maybe ink-black and slightly wavy, like Antonio's, or chestnut-brown and riotous like hers.

Claire wondered if he ever thought of their baby. Did he lie awake at night even now and imagine he could hear her crying? Did his arms ache to hold her just one more time, as hers did every day? Did he look at the last photograph taken of her in the delivery suite and feel an unbearable pain searing through his chest that those tiny eyes had never opened to look at his face?

Probably not, she thought bitterly as she rummaged in her wardrobe for something to wear. She pulled out a black dress and held it up for inspection. It was three or four seasons old, and far too big for her, but what did it matter? She wasn't out to impress him. That was the job of the supermodels and socialites he partied with all over Europe.

CHAPTER TWO

THE HAMMOND TOWER HOTEL was close to the city center, with stunning views over the harbour, and the sail-like wings of the iconic Sydney Opera House visible from some angles. But, unlike the other hotels the Hammond competed with, it had an old-world charm about it; the art deco design and furnishings and the immaculately uniformed attendants made Claire feel as if she was stepping back in time, to a far more gracious and glamorous era that few modern hotels could rival, in spite of their massive stainless steel and glass towers.

Claire left her car with the valet parking man, trying not to wince in embarrassment when the engine coughed and choked behind her as he valiantly tried to get it to move.

The doorman on duty smiled in greeting and held the brass and glass doors open for her. 'Good evening, madam,' he said. 'Welcome to the Hammond.'

'Thank you,' Claire said with a polite smile in return, and made her way towards the plush Piano Bar on legs that felt uncoordinated and treacherously unsteady.

Antonio was sitting on one of the leather sofas and got to his feet when he saw her approach. Claire felt her breath hitch in her throat like a bramble brushing against soft fabric. He was so commandingly tall; how could she have forgotten how petite she'd always felt standing in front of him? He towered over her, his darker than night eyes probing hers without giving anything away.

'Claire.'

That was all he said, just her name, and yet it caused a reaction so intense Claire could barely get her brain to work, let alone her voice. Her gaze consumed him greedily, ravenously, taking in every detail of his features in that pulsing nanosecond of silence. Would he touch her? she wondered in a flash of panic. Should she make the first move so as to keep things on her terms? Or should she lift each cheek in turn for the kiss she had learned was commonplace while living in Italy? Or stand stiffly, as she was doing now, her arms by her sides, the fingers of her right hand tightly clasped around her purse, her heart thumping like a bass drum as she delayed the final moment when she would have to meet his black-as-pitch gaze?

He had barely changed. He still had no signs of grey in his raven-black hair, even though he was now thirty-six years old, and his skin was still tanned, his jaw cleanly shaven. The classic lines of his Italian designer business suit did nothing to hide the superb physical condition he was in. Broad-shouldered and lean-waisted, with long, strong legs and narrow hips—all speaking of a man who took his health and fitness seriously, in spite of the long hours he worked.

'A-Antonio...' She finally managed to speak his

name, but it came out barely audible and distinctly wobbly. She could have kicked herself for revealing how much his presence unsettled her. Why couldn't she be cool and sophisticated for once? Why did she have to feel as if her heart was in a vice, with someone slowly but surely turning the handle until she couldn't breathe?

'Would you like to sit down?' He gestured towards the sofa he had just vacated.

So polite, so formal, Claire thought as she sat down, keeping her legs angled away from his as he resumed his seat.

'What would you like to drink?' he asked as the drinks waiter came over.

'Something soft…mineral water,' she said, clutching her purse against her lower body like a life raft. 'I'm driving.'

Antonio ordered her a mineral water, and a brandy and dry for himself, before he sat back to look at her. 'You have lost weight,' he said.

A spark of irritation came and went in her blue-green eyes. 'Is that a criticism or an observation?' she asked.

'I was not criticising you, Claire.'

She folded her arms in a keep-away-from-me pose. 'Look, can we just get this over with?' she asked. 'Say what you want to say and let me get back to my life.'

'What life would that be, I wonder?' he asked, leaning back, one arm draped casually over the back of the sofa as his dark gaze ran over her lazily.

She narrowed her eyes at him, two points of colour firing in her cheeks. 'I have a life, Antonio, it's just I choose not to have you in it.'

Antonio smiled to himself. She had such a cutting

tongue when she thought she could get away with it. But now he was here he had ways and means to bring her to heel, and bring her to heel he would. 'We have things to discuss, Claire,' he said. 'We have been apart a long time, and some decisions have to be made about where we go from here.'

'I can tell you where we go from here,' she said. 'We go straight to court and formally end our marriage.'

He paused for a moment, taking in her flashing blue-green gaze and the way her soft-as-a-feather-pillow mouth was pulled into a tight line. The skin of her face was a pale shade of cream, with a tiny dusting of freckles over the bridge of her *retroussé* nose, giving her a girl-next-door look that was captivating. He had already noted how every male head had turned when she had come into the bar. She was either totally unaware of the effect she had on the male gaze, or she very cleverly ignored it to enhance her feminine power.

'What if I told you I do not want a divorce?' he said after a measured pause.

She put her mineral water down with a sharp little thwack on the nearest coffee table, her eyes going wide as she stared at him. 'What did you say?'

He gave her an indolent half-smile. 'You heard me.'

She sucked in a breath and threw him a flint-like glare. 'That's too bad, Antonio, because I *do* want one.'

Antonio kept on pinning her with his gaze. 'Then why have you not done anything about it before now?'

She shifted her eyes from his. 'I...I couldn't be bothered,' she muttered in a petulant tone. 'You were out of sight and out of my mind, as far as I was concerned.'

'But now I am back you suddenly want to put an

end to our marriage?' he snapped his fingers. 'Just like that.'

She looked at him with icy disdain. 'Our marriage ended five years ago, Antonio, and you damn well know it.'

'And why was that?' Antonio asked, not bothering to disguise his simmering anger this time. 'Because you wanted to blame someone for anything and everything and I was the nearest scapegoat?'

She glared at him heatedly. He could see a pulse leaping in her neck, and how her fingers were so tight around her purse. Each and every one of her knuckles looked as if the tiny bones were going to break through the fine layer of her skin.

'You betrayed me,' she said in a low hard tone. 'You betrayed me when I was at my lowest point. I will never forgive you for that.'

Antonio clenched his jaw, the pressure making his teeth ache. 'So you are still running with that fairy story about me being unfaithful to you in the last few months of our relationship, are you?'

Her eyes flashed with pure venom. 'I know what I saw,' she hissed at him in an undertone, so the other drinkers in the bar wouldn't hear. 'You were holding her in your arms, so don't bother denying it.'

'I would not dream of denying it,' he said. 'Daniela was and still is a close family friend. You know that. That is something else I told you when we first met.'

'Yes, but you neglected to tell me you were her lover for the eighteen months prior,' she tossed back. 'A minor detail but a rather important one, I would have thought.'

Antonio put his drink down. 'I did not want to upset

you with talk of my ex-lovers,' he said. 'It did not seem appropriate since you were without similar experience.'

'Yes, well, I certainly got all the experience I needed living with you for almost a year,' Claire said, with an embittered set to her mouth.

His eyes warred with hers for a tense moment. 'Why don't you say it, Claire?' he said. 'Why don't you tell everyone in this bar what it is you really blame me for?'

Now she had made him so blisteringly angry Claire wasn't sure she knew how to handle it. She was used to him being cold and distant, clinically detached, with no hint of emotion ever showing through his mask-like expression.

She became aware of the interested glances of the other guests in the bar and felt her face begin to crawl with colour. 'Would you mind keeping your voice down?' she asked in a terse whisper. 'People are staring at us.'

'Let them bloody well stare.'

Claire cringed as she heard someone snicker close by. 'Could we at least go somewhere a little more private?' she said in desperation.

Antonio got to his feet. 'Come with me,' he said, and set a brisk pace towards the lifts situated on the other side of the marbled foyer.

Claire followed at a slower pace, on account of her heels, stepping into the lift he was holding for her, moving to the back of it, as far away from him as the space allowed.

She watched as he swiped his security pass for the penthouse floor, her nerves jumping and leaping beneath her skin as the doors whooshed closed and the lift began to climb each floor.

The silence apart from the mechanical whirr of the lift was palpable; it seemed to grow teeth, snapping at her where she stood in her corner.

Claire could feel her heart thumping irregularly, the blood racing through her veins at breakneck speed. She felt the faint knocking of her knees, and the on-off clench of her insides as the lift finally came to a smooth halt.

Antonio held the doors open for her and she slipped past him, her breath locking in her throat as she caught a faint trace of his lemon-based aftershave, an evocative fragrance that brought a host of memories to the forefront of her brain. Memories of her body pinned beneath his, her skin smelling of him, the taste of him salty and sexy in her mouth, all her muscles relaxed in the afterglow of their shared passion. Each vision made her body glow with heat; she could feel the creep of colour in her cheeks and wondered if he knew what had put it there.

He unlocked the door of his suite with the security card and silently gestured for her to enter, his dark eyes unreadable as they followed her every movement. Claire lowered her gaze and moved past, the gentle swish of her skirt brushing against his trouser legs, making her even more acutely aware of him.

The sound of the door closing behind her made her skin pepper all over with goosebumps, and to disguise her reaction she took a leisurely wander over to the bank of windows, looking down at the view as if that alone was what she was there for.

She sensed him come up behind her, the hairs on the nape of her neck rising to attention one by one. She suppressed a tiny shiver, and concentrated on watching a brightly lit ferry go under the Harbour Bridge.

'So you want a divorce?' he said, as if she was an employee who had just asked for a raise that was not going to be forthcoming.

Claire turned and faced him combatively. 'You can't deny me one, Antonio. We've been separated for too long for you to contest it.'

'I realise that,' he said, holding her gaze with the dark intensity of his. 'And if that is what you want then I will grant you one. But only after the three months of my stay.'

'I'm not sure I'm following you,' she said, frowning at him guardedly. 'Are you suggesting some sort of temporary reconciliation?'

His eyes continued to watch her steadily. 'I would like us to try again, Claire,' he said. 'This time on your territory, not mine.'

Claire felt the stungun-like blows of her heart inside her chest cavity as his words gradually filtered through her brain. 'You're serious about this…aren't you?' she said. 'My God, Antonio, you are out of your mind if you think I would agree to something like that.'

His expression had more than a hint of intractability about it. 'Three months is not a long period of time, Claire,' he said. 'If things do not work out then what has been lost? This way we can both be assured we are making the right decision.'

She sent him a querulous look. 'As far as I am concerned I made the right decision when I caught that plane back home to Sydney.'

'You made that decision in the heat of the moment, after a particularly harrowing time,' he returned.

Claire gaped at him in rapidly rising rage. 'That's

how you refer to her now, is it? "A particularly harrow-ing time"?'

He drew in a breath as he raked a hand through his hair. 'I knew you would be like this,' he said. 'It is im-possible to discuss anything with you without you twisting everything I say to imply I did not care about our daughter. Damn you, Claire, you know that is not true. I wanted her more than anything.'

Claire clenched her jaw, her emotions beginning to spiral out of control. Yes, he *had* wanted their baby; it was just his wife he hadn't wanted as part of the bargain. 'Say her name, for God's sake. Say her name—or have you forgotten it? Is that it, Antonio?' Her voice rose to a shrill level. 'Have you forgotten all about her?'

He set his mouth. 'Do not do this, Claire. It will not bring her back.'

Claire swung away, biting the inside of her mouth to stop herself from becoming hysterical as she had so many times in the past. He was so good at keeping his emotions at bay, which made her loss of control all the more hu-miliating. How she hated him for it. How could he stand there so coldly and impersonally, assuming she would fall in with his plans, as if by crooking his little finger she would run back to him as if nothing had happened?

'I am serious about this trial reconciliation, Claire,' he said into the thrumming silence.

She turned back, her eyes flashing at him defiantly. 'Well, I hate to inform you, Antonio, but you've got your work cut out for you—because the very last thing I will ever agree to is resuming the position of your wife. Not for three months, not for three weeks, not even for three days.'

He gave her a long, studied look, his dark eyes centred on hers. 'You might want to rethink that position after you have spoken with the authorities about the situation one of your half-brothers has just landed himself in.'

Claire felt her eyes rounding in alarm. 'W-which one?' she asked, silently praying it wasn't Isaac. *Oh, please God don't let it be Isaac.* Callum was no angel, having had a few run-ins with the law in the past, but he was on the straight and narrow now. Isaac, however, was the vulnerable one—young and hot-headed, and fiercely loyal at times, which had got him into trouble more often than not.

'Isaac,' Antonio answered.

Claire swallowed, and hoped the despair wasn't showing on her face. 'What has he…um…allegedly done?' she asked with a lift of her chin.

He slanted one brow in a wry manner. 'I see you are no stranger to the legal vernacular when it comes to the behaviour of your sibling.'

She drew in a breath and forced herself to hold his gaze. 'I am the first to admit Isaac has some behavioural issues,' she said. 'But I fail to see what they have to do with you.'

'Actually, his behaviour on this occasion has everything to do with me,' he said, with a purposeful glint in his dark eyes. 'And you too, when it comes to it.'

Don't ask, Claire tried to warn herself, but even so the words left her lips in a stumbling stream. 'What do you mean?'

'Your brother took it upon himself to steal my hire car from the hospital car park earlier this afternoon and take it for a joy-ride,' he said.

Oh, dear God, Claire thought in rising despair. Of all the cars in Sydney, why pick Antonio Marcolini's? She knew Isaac was still in the city; he had come down from the country to go surfing with some friends. He had come to see her only a couple of days ago. He had stayed overnight, and she had given him some money to put towards a new wetsuit.

'Um…was there any damage?' she asked, with a thread of hope holding her voice almost but not quite steady.

'None that three months living with me as my wife will not rectify,' he said, his eyes boring into hers with steely intent.

Claire stared at him, her heart doing a pretty fair imitation of her car's recalcitrant engine on a cold morning. *'You're blackmailing me to come back to you?'* she choked out.

'The word blackmail implies a lack of choice,' he said, with an enigmatic tilt of his lips that was close to a smile. 'In this instance I am giving you a choice, Claire. You either return to our marriage for the duration of my stay in Sydney or I will press charges against your brother. What is it to be?'

CHAPTER THREE

CLAIRE felt the arctic-cold water of shock trickle drop by chilling drop down her spine as she stood gaping speechlessly at the man she had once loved more than life itself. What he was suggesting was unthinkable. But the alternative was even more horrifying. If Isaac went to prison, or even a detention centre, how could she ever forgive herself, knowing she'd had the means to prevent it? Callum had once described some of the things that went on in remand centres, and none of them had anything to do with justice.

But returning to the marriage that had brought her such heartache and unmitigated despair was surely going to test her limits. How on earth would she do it? What strength of character would she need to draw on to see it through?

Hatred clogged her veins as she sent Antonio a castigating glare. 'You've really surpassed yourself this time, Antonio,' she said. 'I thought your callous, unfeeling treatment of me in the past set the benchmark, but this is way above that. You couldn't have thought of a better revenge than this.'

He responded coolly. 'I am merely offering you an escape route which will be of benefit to all parties concerned.'

Claire rolled her eyes again, only because she knew it would annoy him. 'Pardon me,' she said, 'but I fail to see how *I* could possibly benefit from this outrageous plan of yours.'

Anger flickered in his gaze as it pinned hers. 'Have you ever thought of the sort of damage your brother could have done this afternoon?' he asked.

Claire lifted her chin. 'So your precious prestige hire car got a scratch or two? So what?'

His mouth stretched into a thin, flat line of fury. 'Do you have any idea of how many faces I have had to reconstruct over the years?' he ground out. 'Beautiful, perfect faces, permanently damaged by fools like your brother, whose idea of fun is to do burnouts and wheelies in city streets with no thought or regard to whoever else might be on them. That is what my life's work is all about, Claire. Not that you have ever shown a moment's interest, of course.'

'That is just so typical of you,' she threw back. 'I gave up my whole life for you and your career—not that you ever noticed. I was stuck at home day after miserable day, with only your mother and very occasionally your father dropping in just often enough to remind me none too subtly how I wasn't good enough to be their precious firstborn brilliant surgeon son's wife.'

His jaw tightened like a clamp. 'That is not how my mother tells it,' he bit out. 'She tried her utmost to help you settle in, but you refused to give an inch.'

'Here we go again,' Claire said with a curl of her lip.

'Her version and mine—and you still can't make up your mind which one to believe.'

Antonio thrust his hands into his trouser pockets in case he was tempted to pull her into his arms and kiss her into submission. She was so damned infuriating. No one could make him angrier than she did. He was master of his emotions, he always had been—and needed to be during the long hours of complicated surgical proce- dures where a cool, calm head was essential. But five minutes with Claire in this mood was enough to set his blood on the boil.

The very fact she had demanded a divorce the moment he stepped foot in the country showed how much of a gold-digger she had become. He could not stomach her getting half of his inheritance. He would do anything to prevent it. She had already taken enough. It still infuriated him to think of her demanding money from his mother the day she had left him.

Their blazingly hot affair had suddenly changed gear when she had informed him she was carrying his child. He had stood by her, marrying her promptly even though he had always had some misgivings over the true state of her feelings. She had claimed to love him, but he had always suspected it was the lifestyle she had fallen in love with, not him at all. From the little she had told him, he knew she came from a relatively poor back- ground. Money had been scarce and luxuries almost unheard of. She had certainly acted a little starstruck on more than one occasion. Her wide-eyed wonder at the way he and his family lived had amused him at first, but after a while he'd realised he had become a passage for her to a new life, a life where each day wasn't a struggle for survival. That was until fate had stepped in with its most devastating of blows.

Thinking of that time always twisted his insides. He had been so busy, so very distracted. The surgical career pathway was strenuously demanding at the best of times, but juggling the needs of a young wife during an unplanned pregnancy and long hours of study and operating had been crippling, to say the least. His mother had told him many times how she had found Claire still in her dressing gown, moping about the villa, unwilling to make the slightest effort to adjust to being a surgeon's wife. Claire had obviously expected him to be at her beck and call, a nine-to-five sort of husband, when he had been anything but.

His own feelings he hated examining too closely, although he had to admit if he had loved her half as much as he had lusted after her maybe things would have been different. Love was a word he had never been quite comfortable using when it came to Claire, or indeed any other woman he had been involved with. He had decided long ago he was not the falling in love type.

The trouble was he still wanted her. He had never stopped wanting her. It was like a thrumming pulse in his body every time he was near her. His blood pounded in his veins as he thought of the ways she had pleasured him in the past. What she had lacked in experience she had made up for in enthusiasm. He had never had a more satisfying lover. Something about Claire and her responses to him, and his to her, made him feel as if he would never be content until he got her out of his system once and for all. And this was the perfect opportunity to do it.

'Claire,' he said locking his gaze with hers, 'is it

possible for us to put aside the past for a moment and discuss this like mature adults?'

The look she sent him was contemptuous. 'I fail to see what is mature about forcing me back into your life when you didn't want me in it in the first place,' she said. 'All you really wanted was an heir, and I once I failed to provide one you moved on to the next person who could.'

Antonio silently counted to ten to control his temper. 'So I take it your decision is to send your brother to prison? Is that correct?'

She turned away from him, folding her arms across her chest like a shield. 'You know I would do anything to stop that happening,' she said. 'No doubt that's why you're playing that particular card from the deck.'

'This is not a game, Claire.'

She turned to look at him again, her expression cynical. 'Isn't it?'

He blew out a gust of breath. 'I am thirty-six years old,' he said. 'I want to settle down at some point, but I cannot do that until things are finalised between us one way or the other.'

Claire felt a sensation akin to a sharp pain beneath her ribcage. 'So…' She ran her tongue over the sudden dryness of her lips. 'So you're thinking of getting married to someone else…once we get a divorce?'

His eyes gave little away, his expression even less. 'That is not an unlikely scenario,' he answered. 'I have been thinking about it a lot lately.'

'Are you…' Claire swallowed against the aching restriction in her throat. 'Are you planning on having children?'

Again his expression was shuttered, totally and frustratingly unreadable. 'It is a goal of mine, indeed of most people my age, to have a child or two if it is at all possible.'

'Then I'm not sure why you are wasting your time on our relationship, given it has already failed once,' she said, holding his gaze with an effort. 'Wouldn't you be better placed looking for a replacement wife, instead of trying to refashion the one you've got and don't really want?'

'I do not recall saying I did not want you,' he said, with a look that would have ignited tinder. 'On the contrary, you would not be here right now if that was not my primary focus.'

Claire's eyes widened, her heart skipping a beat. 'So…so what you're saying is…you still want me… as in…*sex*?'

A corner of his mouth lifted in a smile that set her pulse racing out of control. 'You find that surprising, *cara*?' he asked.

'Actually, I find it totally insulting,' she tossed back, desperate to disguise her reaction to him. 'You haven't spoken to me in five years, other than via an occasional terse e-mail in the first few months of our separation, and now you're expecting me to dive headfirst into your bed. What sort of woman do you think I am to agree to something as deplorable as that?'

'You do not have a current lover, so I do not see why this will not work between us—for the time being at least.'

Claire narrowed her eyes in outrage. 'How do you know I don't have a lover? Have you done some sort of background search on me?'

'You are still legally married to me, Claire,' he said. 'I believe it is very much my business to know if you are involved with anyone at present. Particularly if we are to resume a physical relationship.'

'That is a very big if,' she said, folding her arms. 'Anyway, what about you? How many women have *you* had during our separation?'

'I have had the occasional date, but nothing serious.'

Claire wanted to believe him, but knowing him as she did, or at least had, she couldn't imagine him remaining celibate for five years. He was a full-blooded male, healthy and virile, with a sex drive that had left her shuddering in his arms each and every time. She could feel that virility and potency now. The sensual spell he cast was woven around her like an invisible mist. She couldn't see it but she could feel it dampening her skin, making her aware of his maleness as no one else could. She could feel her breasts stirring against the lace of her bra, the tightness of her nipples reminding her of how his hot, moist mouth had suckled on her, his teeth tugging at her in playful little bites that had made her toes curl. Her belly quivered, the hollow ache of her womanhood pulsing with longing to be filled with his length and thickness again and again, driving her to the cataclysmic release she had silently craved for every one of the days, months and years they had spent apart.

It shamed her to be confronted by her own weakness where he was concerned. What sort of gullible fool would she be to go back for a second helping of betrayal and heartbreak?

He had never wanted their relationship to be anything other than a short-term affair, but her accidental pregnancy had changed everything. It had taken her almost a month to summon up the courage to tell him. Claire still remembered the total look of shock on his face when she had. But then to her surprise he had insisted they get married. It was only later she'd realised it had not been because he loved her, but because he had wanted an heir.

Claire had always known Antonio wasn't anywhere near as serious about her as she was about him. She had heard the adage far too many times to ignore it: Italian men slept with foreigners, but when it came to settling down they married their own countrywomen. But even so she had been caught up in the fairytale of it all: having a handsome man who lavished her with gifts and took her on exciting dates, not to mention one who initiated her into the heady pleasures of the flesh. It was all like a dream come true to a shy country girl from the Outback of Australia.

Claire had always been so careful with men in the past. She hadn't wanted to repeat the mistakes of her mother, pregnant and abandoned at a young age, spending most of her life looking for love in all the wrong places, and going on to have two other children, none of whose fathers had stayed around long enough to have their names registered on the birth certificates.

Claire hadn't slept around like most of her peers. Instead she had saved up the money from the three part-time jobs she'd juggled in order to put herself through hairdressing college. She had graduated as student of the year, and spent the next year or so saving for a holiday abroad, wanting to see the world before she settled into an upmarket salon.

But then she had met Antonio.

He had come in for a haircut, and as Riccardo, her

flamboyant boss, had been double-booked due to a mistake one of the apprentices had made, he had asked her to wash and cut Antonio's hair for him.

Claire had smiled up at the tall, gorgeous-looking man, introducing herself shyly. 'I am so sorry about the mistake in the appointment book,' she said. 'Riccardo has spoken to you about me filling in for him?'

Antonio smiled. 'It is not a problem,' he said. 'You are from England, *si*?'

'No.' She felt herself blushing and gushing. 'I'm actually Australian, from Sydney…well, really the country, not the city…a rural district…you know…cows and sheep…that sort of thing.'

'Ah, Australia,' he said, taking the chair she held out for him. 'I have distant relatives there. In fact my younger brother has been there several times. I have been promising myself a trip out there some time. It is the land of opportunities, *si*?'

Claire draped the cape around his impossibly broad shoulders, her nerves fizzing as her fingers accidentally came into contact with the raspy skin along his jaw. 'Um…yes…I guess so. If you're prepared to work hard,' she said, trying to avoid meeting his coal-black eyes in the mirror.

'Do you speak Italian?'

'*Non parlo Italiano,*' she said with an apologetic grimace. 'But I would like to learn. I've been thinking about taking some classes.'

He met her eyes in the mirror and held them. 'I will give you a lesson for free if you agree to have dinner with me tonight.'

Claire's fingers stilled amongst the silky strands of his

sooty black hair. 'Um…I'm not sure if Riccardo agrees with his staff fraternising with clients,' she faltered.

'He will agree when it comes to me,' Antonio said, with the sort of easy confidence that would have presented itself as arrogance in anyone else.

'Would you like to come over to the basin?' she asked, trying for cool and calm but not quite pulling it off.

Antonio rose from the chair, his height yet again dwarfing her. 'Riccardo must think a lot of your skill if he has shunted one of his best clients into your hands,' he said. 'Will I be safe?'

Claire responded to his flirting as any other young woman would have done. 'Only if you behave yourself, Signor Marcolini,' she said with a smile. 'I make a habit of keeping all of my customers satisfied—even the most demanding ones.'

'I am sure you do,' he said, and put back his head so she could wash his hair.

Claire had to drag herself out of the past to concentrate on the here and now. She didn't want to remember how it had felt to run her fingers through his hair, to massage his scalp for far longer than any other client before or since. She didn't want to remember how she had agreed to have dinner with him—not just that night but the following night as well. And she certainly didn't want to remember the way he had kissed her on their third date, his mouth sending her into a frenzy of want that had led to her lying naked in his arms only moments later, his body plunging into hers, her muffled cry of discomfort bringing him up short, shocked, horrified that he had inadvertently hurt her…

No. Claire shoved the memories back even further. It

had been the first time he had hurt her, but not the last. And there was no way she was going to think about the last.

'I find it hard to believe you have been without a regular bedmate for the last five years,' she said, voicing her doubts out loud.

'Believe what you like,' he said. 'As in the past, I have no control over the unfathomable workings of your mind.'

Claire ground her teeth. 'You know, you are really going to have to dig a little deeper on the charm front to get me back into your bed, Antonio.'

He gave her an imperious smile. 'You think?'

She took a step backwards, her hands clenched into fists by her sides. 'What do your parents and brother think of your dastardly little scheme to lure me back into the fold of the Marcolini family?'

A shadow passed through his dark eyes. It was just a momentary, almost fleeting thing, and Claire thought how she could so easily have missed it. 'My father unfortunately passed away a couple of months ago,' he said, with little trace of emotion in his voice. 'He had a massive heart attack. Too many cigarettes, too much stress, and not enough advice taken from his doctors or his family to slow down, I am afraid.' He paused for a moment, his dark eyes pinning hers in a disquieting manner. 'I thought you would have read about it in the press?'

'I…I must have missed it,' she said, lowering her voice and her gaze respectfully. 'I am so sorry. Your mother must miss him greatly. You must all miss him…'

'My mother is doing the best she can under the circumstances,' he said after another slight pause. 'My brother Mario has taken over my father's business.'

Claire brought her gaze back to his in surprise.

'What? You mean your father didn't leave you anything in his will?'

An indefinable look came into his eyes. 'Mario and I are both partners in the business, of course, but due to my career commitments I have by necessity left most of the corporate side of things to him.'

'I am sure your brother was shocked to hear of your intention to look me up while you are here,' Claire commented with a wry look.

Antonio continued to hold her look with an inscrutable one of his own. 'I have spoken to my brother, who told me rather bluntly he thinks I am a fool for even considering a rematch with you. But then he has always been of the philosophy of one strike and you are out. I am a little more...how shall I say...accommodating?'

Claire could just imagine his playboy younger brother bad-mouthing her to Antonio. His parents had been the same—not that Antonio would ever believe it. That last degrading scene with his mother had been filed away in Claire's do-not-go-there-again-file in her head. She had kept the cheque in her purse for weeks, folded into a tiny square, frayed at the edges, just as her temper was every time she thought of how she had been dismissed, like a servant who hadn't fulfilled the impossible expectations of her employer. But then she had finally cashed it, without a twinge of conscience. As far as she was concerned it had been money well spent.

'How do you know it was my brother who took your car?' Claire asked, looking at Antonio warily. 'You've never met any of my family.' *Thank God*, she thought. What he would make of her loving but totally unsophisticated mother was anyone's guess, but her brothers—

as much as she loved them—were way beyond the highbrow circles Antonio moved in.

'When the police caught him he identified himself,' Antonio said. 'He made no effort at all to cover up the fact he was my young brother-in-law.'

Claire felt her stomach drop.

'Wh-where is he?' she asked. 'Where is my brother now?'

'I have arranged for him to spend a few days with a friend of mine,' he said. 'He runs a centre for troubled youths on the South Coast.'

She clenched her fists by her sides. 'I want to see him. I want to see my brother to make sure he's all right.'

'I will organise for you to speak to him via the telephone,' he said, and reached for his mobile.

Claire sank her teeth into her bottom lip as she listened to him speak to his friend before he handed her the phone. She took it with a shaking hand and held it up to her ear, turning away so he wouldn't see the anguish on her face, nor hear what her brother had to say.

'Isaac? It's me, Claire.'

'Yo, sis. What's up?'

Claire mentally pinched the bridge of her nose. 'I think you know what's up,' she said, stepping further out of Antonio's hearing and keeping her voice low. 'Why did you do it, Isaac? Why on earth did you take Antonio Marcolini's car?'

Her brother muttered a filthy swear word. 'I hate the way he treated you. I thought it would help. Why should he drive around in such a cool-dude car when yours is a heap of rust?' he asked. 'Rich bastard. Anyway, I thought you were going to divorce him?'

Claire cringed as the sound of her brother's voice carried across the room. Turning away from Antonio's livid dark brown gaze, she said, 'I'm actually considering…um…getting back with him.'

Her brother let out another swear word. 'Get *out*. Jeez, why didn't you tell me that the other day?'

'Would it have made a difference?' she asked.

There was a small silence.

'Yeah…maybe…I dunno. You seemed pretty cut up about that article and the photo in the paper.'

Claire squeezed her eyes shut. Why hadn't she thrown it in the rubbish, where it belonged? 'Look, I just want you to promise me you'll behave yourself now you've been given this chance.'

'Don't 'ave much choice, locked up here,' he grumbled.

Claire frowned. 'You're locked up?'

'Well…sort of,' Isaac said. 'It's some sort of youth reform centre. It's kind of all right, though. The food's OK, and they've given me a room to myself and a TV. The head honcho wants me to think about teaching some of the kids to surf. I might take it on; I've got nothing better to do.'

'Just stay there and do as you're told, Isaac,' she pleaded with him.

'So you're dead serious about getting back with the Marcolini bloke, huh?' Isaac asked.

She lowered her voice even further, but even so it seemed to echo ominously off the walls of the plush suite—just as her brother's damning words had. 'Yes,' she said. 'I am as of this moment going to return to Antonio and live with him as his wife.'

CHAPTER FOUR

CLAIRE handed back Antonio's phone with a look of grim resignation on her face. 'Would you like me to lie down on the bed now, so you can get straight down to business?' she asked. 'Or would you like me to perform a strip show and really get your money's worth?'

Anger flared like a struck match in his dark eyes. 'There is no need to prostitute yourself, Claire,' he said. 'We will resume a physical relationship only when I am convinced it is what we both want. Right at this moment I can see you would much rather rake your nails down my face than anything else.'

Claire felt relief tussling with her disappointment, making her feel disconcerted over what it was she actually felt for Antonio. She had told herself so many times how much she hated him, and yet standing before him now she found that hatred proving frustratingly elusive. Other feelings had crept up on her—dangerous feelings of want and need. She could feel the traitorous beat of her pulse, the hit and miss of her heartbeats reminding her of the sensual power he still had over her.

'So…' She tried to keep her voice steady and her expression coolly detached. 'This three-month reconciliation… Am I supposed to move in here with you, or do I get to keep my own place?'

'You are renting at present? Is that correct?' he asked.

Claire wondered again how he knew so much about her current circumstances when their contact had been so limited. In the first weeks after she had left he had called and left message after message on her mobile, but she had deleted them without listening. He had e-mailed her several times, but she had not responded, and in the end had changed her e-mail address and her mobile number. She had assured herself if he really wanted to contact her he would find some way of doing so. But after some months had gone by, and then a couple of years, and then another couple, she'd resigned herself to the fact he had well and truly moved on.

'Claire?'

'Um…yes,' she said. 'I'm renting a place in Glebe, not far from the salon.'

'Do you own the salon outright?'

She frowned at him. 'What, do you think I am made of money or something?' she asked. 'Of course I don't own it outright. I work for a friend, Rebecca Collins.'

Antonio searched her features for a moment. 'So if you do not own a share in the salon, and you rent where you live, what exactly did you do with the money my mother gave you?' he asked.

Her shoulders went back and her blue-green eyes flashed flick knives of resentment at him. 'So she told you about that, did she?' she asked.

'She reluctantly informed me of it a couple of weeks after you left,' he said, keeping his expression deliberately shuttered.

'I looked upon it as a severance payout,' she said. 'After all, you no longer required my services once you'd hooked back up with Daniela Garza.'

Antonio ignored that little jibe to ask, 'Is that why you refused to accept money from me, even though I offered it repeatedly in my e-mails and phone calls?'

She gave him another castigating glare. 'Do you really think I would have accepted money from you after what you did?' she asked.

His lip curled in disdain. 'And yet you demanded it from my mother.'

Shocked, she stared at him with wide eyes. '*What* did you say?'

He let a three beats of silence pass.

'I think you heard what I said, Claire,' he said. 'You blackmailed my mother, forcing her to pay you a large sum of money to stop you going to the press about your marriage to me.'

She was looking at him as if he was speaking another language. But Antonio was well aware of how manipulative she could be, and still had his suspicions about her plans to take him for what she could get. Yet no one looking at her now would think her guilty of such a scheme. Her eyes were wide, feigning shocked innocence, her mouth trembling and her face pale.

'You have not answered my question,' he said.

Her back visibly stiffened, although her tone sounded calm and even. 'What question is that?'

'What did you do with the money?'

She let out her breath in a long hissing stream. 'What do you think I did with it?'

He frowned at her darkly. 'I would have given you money, damn it, Claire. But you always refused it.'

She turned her back on him. 'It was less personal taking it from her,' she said. 'I didn't want anything to do with you.'

'So what did you do with it?'

She turned after a moment, her expression as cold as the night air outside. 'I spent it on myself,' she said, with that same razor-sharp glint in her eyes. 'That's what gold-diggers do, isn't it, Antonio?'

He drew in a breath as he reined back his temper. She was deliberately goading him, as she had done so many times before. Yes, he had proof she had blackmailed his mother, even though she now staunchly denied it, but he understood how she would have seen it as some sort of payback for him not being there for her in the way she had wanted him to be.

He had come to a time in his life now where he wanted to put down roots. His father's sudden death had no doubt got a lot to do with it—not to mention his mother's deterioration since. And, since his brother Mario had no intention of settling down and producing a Marcolini heir, it was up to Antonio to make some important decisions about his own future. He could not move on until he had tied up the loose and frayed ends of the past. God knew he owed it to his beautiful little daughter, who hadn't even had the chance to take her first breath.

Antonio swallowed against the avalanche of emotion he felt whenever he pictured that tiny, perfect, lifeless face. He had helped so many people during the long, arduous course of his surgical career. He had saved lives, he had changed lives, he had restored health and vitality to people who had stared death or disfigurement in the face—and yet he had not been there when his daughter and Claire had needed him most.

It tortured him to think he might have been able to do something. Claire had gone into labour far too early. He had ignored the signs when she had mentioned her concerns that morning. He had no excuse, not really. The truth was he had been distracted with the case scheduled first on his list that day. A young girl of only seventeen, who had just landed herself a lucrative modelling contract, had been involved in a horrific traffic accident some weeks earlier. Antonio hadn't seen anyone quite so damaged before. He'd had to concentrate on preserving crucial facial nerves during surgery that would decide whether she would ever smile her beautiful smile at the camera again. He had perspired beneath his surgical scrubs; it had run like a river down his back as he'd worked with his dedicated team for twelve, nearly thirteen hours, to put her face back together the best they could—hoping, praying she would still be able to live the life she had mapped out for herself.

And he had done it. Bianca Abraggio was still modelling today—her face her fortune, her gorgeous smile intact, her life on track, while Antonio's was still in limbo.

'I do not recall referring to you at any time as a gold-digger,' he said.

She lifted her chin, her eyes flashing at him like shards of blue-green glass. 'You didn't need to. Your family made it more than clear that's what they thought I was.'

'Look,' he said, dragging a hand through his hair, 'I admit they were not expecting me to produce a daughter-in-law for them quite so soon. I was in the middle of my final fellowship training and—'

She cut him off. 'They never accepted me. They thought I wasn't good enough for you. I was a foreigner. I couldn't even speak their language. Not to mention I spoke with a broad Australian accent.'

'That is not true,' Antonio said. He had seen time and time again how both of his parents had tried their level best to get on with Claire, but she had been so fiercely independent they had eventually given up trying to include her. 'Anyway, it was not up to them, it was up to me who I spent my time with. It is still up to me.'

'What would *you* know of how it was for me?' she asked. 'I couldn't bear going through it all again. It has taken me this long to move on.'

Antonio could feel his frustration building, and couldn't quite disguise it in his tone. 'Get used to it, Claire, because you and I are going to spend the next three months together—otherwise you will be personally responsible for sending your brother to jail where he belongs.'

She glared at him furiously. 'I thought you had devoted your life to saving the lives of others?' she said. 'If you send my brother to prison you might as well be signing your name on his death certificate. He won't last a day inside. He'll get bullied or beaten up or something. I know he will.'

The look he gave her was merciless. 'Then do not make me do it, Claire, for I will if I have to. It is in your hands. Do not forget that.'

She threw him a hateful glare as she snatched up her

purse from where she had flung it earlier. Fighting to control her anger was like trying to rein in a bolting horse with nothing but piece of string. She had never thought it was possible to hate someone so intensely—especially someone she had loved so much before. Antonio was a ruthless stranger now, a man without mercy, a man who was prepared to go to unbelievable lengths to have her bend to his will.

'When do you wish to start this ridiculous charade?' she asked.

'Have you had dinner?' he asked.

'Um…no, but I'm not hungry.'

'There is a very fine restaurant within a block of here,' he said. 'I suggest we have dinner together, so as to ease back into our relationship.'

'I don't think I could eat a thing.'

'It looks like you have not eaten a thing in days.'

She gave him a cutting look. 'Is there anything else you would like to criticise me about while you're at it?' she asked.

Antonio's eyes glittered determinedly as they held hers. 'One thing I would like to make very clear from the outset,' he said. 'You can say what you like to me when we are alone, but while we are in the presence of other people I expect you to act with the dignity and decorum befitting your role as my wife.'

'Yes, well, that's all it's going to be,' she snipped back. 'An act—and not a particularly attractive one.'

'I will make sure there are certain compensations,' he said. 'A generous allowance, for one thing, which will mean you can cut back your hours at work—or quit altogether while I am here.'

She stood as stiff as a broom handle. 'You can keep your stupid allowance, and I am *not* giving up my job for you,' she said. 'I want to maintain some element of independence.'

'If that is what you want then I have no issue with it,' he said. 'I just thought you might be glad of a break from the long hours you work. You certainly look like you could do with one.'

Claire knew she had dark shadows under her eyes, and she was at least a couple of kilos lighter than she should be, but did he *have* to make her feel as if she had just crawled out from beneath a rock?

'Would you like me to get a paper bag to place over my head before we are seen in public together?' she asked. 'No doubt I fall rather short of the glamorous standard of the legions of other women you have enjoyed over the last five years.'

He held her challenging look for a tense moment. 'I was merely commenting on how stressed and tired you look, *il mio amato*,' he said. 'There is no need to feel as if everything I say to you is a veiled insult.'

Claire had to hastily swallow to keep her emotions in check. Her heart recognised the term of endearment and swelled in response. *My beloved one.* Of course he didn't mean it. How could he? He had never said he loved her. He had not once revealed anything of how he felt about her apart from at the start of their affair, when his desire for her had been so hot and strong it had left her spinning in its wake.

But then he had left her grieving the loss of their baby to find solace in his previous lover's arms. He had always denied it strenuously, and she might have believed his version of events if it hadn't been for Antonio's mother Rosina confirming her son's clandestine relationship.

'Do we have to do this tonight?' she asked now, with a hint of petulance. 'Why can't we meet for dinner tomorrow, or even the day after?'

'Because I have limited time available,' he said. 'I have a large operating list tomorrow, which could well go over time. And besides, I know what you will do if I give you a reprieve. You will more than likely disappear for the next three months so as to avoid further contact with me.'

Claire shifted her gaze so he wouldn't see how close his assessment of her had been. She had been madly thinking of various escape routes, mentally tallying the meagre contents of her bank account to figure a way of covering her tracks until he left the country. But she could hardly leave Rebecca in the lurch—not after she had always been so supportive of her over the years.

'I know how your mind works, Claire,' he said into the silence. 'You would rather walk over hot coals than spend an evening with me, would you not?'

Claire returned her gaze to his, surprised at the bitterness in his tone. What did *he* have to be bitter about? She hadn't destroyed their marriage, he had—and irreparably. 'You surely don't expect me to be doing cartwheels of joy about you forcing your way back into my life, do you?' she asked.

The line of his mouth tightened. 'I can see why you have lost so much weight,' he said. 'It is no doubt due to that chip on your shoulder you are carrying around.'

Claire gripped her purse so tightly her fingers began

to ache. 'You don't think I have a right to be upset?' she asked. 'I'm not an emotional cardboard cut-out like you, Antonio. I feel, and I feel deeply. Not a day goes past when I don't think about her—about how old she would be now, what she would look like, the things she would be saying and doing. Do you even spare her a single thought?'

His eyes darkened, and the tension around his mouth increased, making a tiny nerve flicker beneath the skin of his rigid jaw. 'I think of her,' he said, his voice sounding as if it had been scraped across a serrated surface. 'Of course I think about her.'

Claire bit the inside of her mouth until she tasted the metallic sourness of blood. She didn't want to break down in front of him. She didn't want him to see how truly vulnerable she still was around him. If he reached out to comfort her she would betray herself; she was sure of it. Her arms would snake around his neck; her body would press up against his in search of the warmth and strength only he could give. Her flesh would spring to life, every cell in her body recognising the magnet-ism of his, drawing her into his sensual orbit, luring her into lowering her guard until she had no defences left. The sooner she was out of this suite and in a public place the better, she decided firmly.

She drew in a scratchy breath and forced herself to meet his gaze. 'I guess dinner would be OK,' she said. 'I missed lunch, and breakfast seems like a long time ago.'

He picked up the security card and slid it into his wallet. 'I will not keep you up too late, Claire. I am still getting over my jet lag.'

Claire noticed then how tired he looked. His dark eyes

were underscored with bruise-like shadows, and the grooves either side of his mouth looked deeper than usual. He still looked as heart-stoppingly gorgeous as ever—perhaps even more so. Maybe it was because she hadn't seen him for so long. She had forgotten how compelling his chocolate-brown eyes were, how thick and sooty his long lashes, and how his beautifully sculpted mouth with its fuller bottom lip hinted at the passion and potency she had tasted there time and time again.

She had to wrench her gaze away from his mouth, where it had drifted of its own volition.

'So…what's this restaurant like?' she asked as they made their way out of his penthouse. 'What sort of cuisine do they offer?'

He reached past her to press the call button for the lift, and Claire felt her breath come to a stumbling halt in her chest. The near brush of his arm had triggered every nerve in her body, until she could almost sense how it would feel to have him touch her again. Her breasts ached for the press of his hands, the brush of his lips, the sweet hot suck of his mouth and the roll and glide and tortuous tease of his tongue. Was she so pleasure-starved as to be suddenly craving the touch of a man she hated? Her mind was playing tricks on her, surely? He had accused her of blackmail, and yet she couldn't quite stop her heart from skipping a beat every time his gaze meshed with hers.

The lift arrived with an almost soundless swish of doors opening, and Claire stepped in, moving to the back, out of temptation's way.

'Come here, Claire,' Antonio commanded.

Claire held her purse like a shield against her traitorous pelvis, where a pulse had begun beating. 'Why?' she asked. 'There's no one else in the lift.'

'No, but as soon as we hit the ground floor there will be. So it is better to start as we mean to go on,' he said.

She frowned at him as suspicion began to crawl beneath her skin. 'How do you know there will be someone there?' she asked.

He held her narrowed gaze with equanimity. 'I took the liberty of releasing a press statement earlier today.'

Claire felt anger rise up within her like a cold, hard substance, stiffening every vertebra of her spine. 'You were *that* sure I would agree to this farce?' she asked.

His eyes glinted as they held hers. 'I was sure you would not like to see your brother face the authorities. I was also sure you would do it for the money.'

The despair she felt at that moment almost consumed her. It was so hurtful to realise how badly he thought of her, how for all this time he'd believed her to be an avaricious opportunist, when all she had ever wanted from him was his love. How could he have got it so wrong about her? Hadn't he seen how much she had adored him? Claire knew she had been a little goggle-eyed at his lifestyle to begin with, but as their relationship had progressed she'd thought she had demonstrated how little his fame and fortune meant to her. Was his heart so hard and impenetrable he was unable to recognise genuine love when he saw it?

'Come here, Claire,' he commanded again, holding out his hand for her.

Claire released her tightly held breath and pressed herself away from the back of the lift, where she had flattened her spine. She took his hand, struggling to hide the way his fingers curling around hers affected her. His hands—his so very clever, life-saving hands—felt strong and warm against hers. They had been one of the first things she had noticed about him all those years ago in Riccardo's salon. Antonio had strong, capable hands—tanned, lightly sprinkled with hair, broad and yet long-fingered, his nails cut short and scrupulously clean from the hundreds of washes he subjected them to in order to operate.

She looked down at their entwined fingers and suppressed a tiny shiver. Those hands had explored every inch of her body. They had known her intimately; they had taught her everything she knew about sexual response. She could feel the warmth of him seeping through her skin, layer by layer, melting the ice of her resolve to keep herself distanced and unaffected by him.

The lift doors opened and a camera flashed in Claire's face as she stepped out hand in hand with Antonio. She cringed, and shielded her eyes from the over-bright glare, but within seconds another journalist had rushed up and thrust a microphone towards her.

'Mrs Marcolini,' the young woman said, struggling to keep up with Antonio's determined stride as he pulled Claire towards the front of the hotel. 'Is it true you are returning to your husband after a five-year estrangement?'

Antonio gently but firmly moved the microphone away from Claire's face. 'Do you mind giving my wife some space?' he asked.

The journalist took this as encouragement, and directed her line of questioning at him instead. 'Mr Marcolini, you are reputed to be here in Sydney for a limited time. Does that mean your new relationship with your wife will be on a set time-frame as well? Or do you intend to take her back to Italy with you once your lecture and surgical tour here in Sydney is completed?'

Claire looked up at Antonio, her breath catching in her throat, but he was as cool and collected as usual, the urbane smile in place, his inscrutable gaze giving no clue to what was ticking over in his mind.

'That is between my wife and I,' he answered. 'We have only just sorted out our differences. Please give us some space and privacy in which to work on our reconciliation.'

'Mr Marcolini.' The young female journalist was clearly undaunted by his somewhat terse response. 'You and your wife suffered the tragedy of a stillbirth five years ago. Do you have any advice to parents who have suffered the same?'

Claire felt the sudden tension in Antonio's fingers where they were wrapped around hers. She looked up at him again, her heart in her throat and the pain in the middle of her chest so severe she could scarcely draw in a much needed breath.

'The loss of a child at any age is a travesty of nature,' he answered. 'Each person must deal with it in their own way and in their own time. There is no blueprint for grief.'

'And you, Mrs Marcolini?' The journalist aimed her microphone back at Claire. 'What advice would you give to grieving parents, having been through it personally?'

Claire stammered her response, conscious there were women out there just like her, who had been torn apart by the loss of a baby and would no doubt be hanging on every word she said. 'Um…just to keep hoping that one day enough research will be done to make sure stillbirths are a thing of the past. And to remember it's not the mother's fault. Things go wrong, even at the last minute. You mustn't blame yourself…that is the important thing. You mustn't blame yourself…'

Antonio, keeping Claire close, elbowed his way through the knot of people and cameras. 'Just keep walking, *cara*,' he said. 'This will die down in a day or two.'

'I can't see why our situation warrants the attention it's just received. Who gives a toss whether we resume our marriage or not? It's hardly headline material.'

Antonio kept her hand tucked in close to his side as he led the way down the sidewalk to the restaurant he had booked earlier. 'Maybe not here in Australia,' he said. 'However, there are newshounds who relay gossip back to Italy from all over the world. They like to document whatever Mario and I do—especially now we are at the helm of the Marcolini empire.'

'So what is Mario up to these days?' Claire asked, not really out of interest but more out of a desire to steer the conversation away from their unusual situation. 'Still flirting with any woman with a pulse?'

Antonio's smile this time was crooked with affection for his sibling. 'You know my brother Mario. He likes to work hard and to play even harder. I believe there is lately someone he is interested in—an Australian girl, apparently, someone he met last time he was here—but so far she has resisted his charm.'

'Yes, well, maybe he could try a little ruthlessness or blackmail,' she said. 'Both seem to run rather freely in the Marcolini family veins.'

He turned to face her, holding her by the upper arms so she couldn't move away. 'I gave you a choice, Claire,' he said, pinning her gaze with his. 'Your freedom or your brother's. You see it as blackmail, I see it as a chance to sort out what went wrong between us.'

She wrenched herself out of his hold, dusting off her arms as if he had tainted her with his touch. 'I can tell you what went wrong with us, Antonio,' she said. 'All I ever was to you was a temporary diversion—someone to warm your bed occasionally. You had no emotional investment in our relationship until there was the prospect of an heir. The baby was a bonus, and once she was out of the equation, so was I.'

Antonio clenched and unclenched his fingers where hers had so recently been. He could still feel the tingling sensation running up under his skin. 'I fulfilled my responsibilities towards you as best I could, but it was never enough for you. So many men in my place would not have done so. Have you ever thought of that? I stood by you and supported you, but you wanted me to be something I am not nor ever could be.'

She sank her teeth into her lip when it began to tremble. Moisture was starting to shine in the blue-green pools of her eyes, making him feel like an unfeeling brute for raising his voice at her. How on earth did she do it to him? One wounded look from her, just one slight wobble of her chin, and he felt the gut-wrenching blows of guilt assail him all over again.

He let out a weighty sigh and captured her hand again, bringing it up to his mouth, pressing his lips warmly against her cold, thin fingers. 'I am sorry, *cara*,' he said gently. 'I do not want to fight with you. We are supposed to be mending bridges, *si*?'

She looked at him for a stretching moment, her eyes still glistening with unshed tears. 'Some bridges can never be mended, Antonio,' she said, pulling her hand out of his.

Antonio held the restaurant door open for her. *Let's just see about that*, he thought with grim determination, and followed her inside.

CHAPTER FIVE

A FEW minutes later, once they were seated at a secluded table with drinks, crusty bread rolls and a tiny dish of freshly pressed olive oil placed in front of them, Claire began to feel the tension in her shoulders slowly dissipate. She could see Antonio was making every effort to put her at ease. His manner towards her had subtly changed ever since that tense moment outside the restaurant.

The earlier interaction with the press had upset him much more than she had thought it would. He was well used to handling the intrusive questions of the paparazzi, but this time she had felt the tensile strain in him as he had tried to protect her. It had touched her that he had done so, and made her wonder if his motives for their reconciliation were perhaps more noble than she had first thought.

The waiter took their orders, and once he had left them Antonio caught and held Claire's gaze. 'Did you blame yourself, Claire?' he asked, looking at her with dark intensity.

Claire pressed her lips together, her eyes falling away

from his to stare at the vertical necklaces of bubbles in her soda water. 'I don't suppose there is a mother anywhere in the world who doesn't feel guilty about the death of her child,' she said sadly.

He reached for her hand across the table, his long, strong fingers interlocking with hers. 'I should have arranged some counselling for you,' he said, in a tone deep with regret.

Claire brought her eyes back to his. 'Would you have come to the sessions as well?'

His eyes shifted to look at the contents of his glass, just as hers had done a moment or so earlier. 'I am used to dealing with life and death, Claire,' he said, briefly returning his gaze to hers. 'I lost my first patient, or at least the first one I was personally responsible for under my care, when I was a young registrar. It was unexpected and not my fault, but I blamed myself. I wanted to quit. I did not think I could carry on with my training. But my professor of surgery at the time took me to one side and reassured me that a surgeon is not God. We do what we can to save and preserve lives, but sometimes things go wrong. Things we have no control over.'

'Is that why you chose plastic surgery rather than general surgery?' Claire asked, wondering why she had never thought to ask him that before.

'I was never really interested in plastics as such,' he answered. 'I understand how many people are unhappy with the features they are born with, and I fully support them seeking help if and where it is appropriate, but I never saw myself doing straight rhinoplasty or breast augmentations or liposuction. Reconstructive work has always appealed to me.

Seeing someone disfigured by an accident or birth defect reclaiming their life and their place in the world is tremendously satisfying.'

'I've seen some of the work you've done on your website,' Claire said. 'The before and after shots are truly amazing.'

He picked up his glass, his expression somewhere between quizzical and wry. 'I am surprised you bothered looking at all. I thought you wanted me out of sight and out of mind.'

She twisted her mouth. 'I guess intrigue got the better of me. From being an overworked registrar when we met to what you are now—a world leader in reconstructive surgery... Well, that's a pretty big leap, and one I imagine you might not have achieved if I had stayed around.'

A frown tugged at his dark brows. 'That seems a rather negative way of viewing yourself,' he said. 'The early years of surgery are punishing, Claire. You know that. It is like any other demanding profession. You have to put in the hard yards before you reap any of the rewards.'

'I suppose some of the rewards, besides the financial ones, are the hordes of women who trail after you so devotedly,' she put in resentfully.

He made an impatient sound at the back of his throat. 'You really are determined to pick a fight every chance you get, are you not? Well, if it is a fight you want, you can have one—but not here and not now. I refuse to trade insults with you over a table in a public restaurant.'

Claire twisted her hands beneath the table, her stomach tightening into familiar knots. 'I don't see that it is necessary for me to move in with you,' she said, nervously moistening her dry lips. 'Surely we can just see how it goes from day to day? You know…go on the occasional date or something, to see if things work out.'

He looked at her with wry amusement. 'Come now, Claire, surely we have moved well past the dating stage, hmm? You have shared my bed and my body in the past. I am quite sure you will not find it too difficult to do so again, especially since there is financial gain to be had.'

Claire had to look away from his taunting gaze. She felt shattered by his chilling assessment of her. He was treating her like a gold-digger, someone who would sleep with him for whatever she could get out of the arrangement. 'I don't want your money,' she said stiffly. 'I have never wanted it.'

He put his glass down so heavily the red wine splashed against the sides, almost spilling over the rim. 'That is not quite true, though, is it, Claire?'

She twisted her hands even more tightly together, forcing herself to hold his accusatory gaze. 'I wanted your time,' she said. 'But you were always too busy to give it to me.'

'I gave you what I could, Claire,' he said, frowning at her darkly. 'I know it was not enough. You did not always get the best of me; my patients back then and now still have that privilege. Most truly dedicated specialists feel the same way. We have lives in our hands. It is a huge responsibility, for they are all someone's son or daughter, husband or wife, brother or sister.'

'What about your own daughter, Antonio?' she asked, tears filling her eyes. 'The specialist you recommended I see failed to get there on time, and so did you. I felt let down. You both let our baby down.'

Antonio hated going over this. They had done it so

many times in the past and it had achieved nothing. All it did was stir up a hornets' nest of guilt in his gut. 'Leave it, Claire,' he said. 'We have to let the past go and move forward. It is the only hope we have to get things right this time around.'

Claire pushed her barely touched food away. 'We wouldn't even be sitting here now if I hadn't asked you for a divorce. You couldn't stand the fact that I'd got in first—just like you couldn't stand the fact that I was the one who left you, not the other way round. And now you have the audacity to use my brother to blackmail me into being with you. I can't believe how ruthless you have become.'

'Your brother has nothing to do with this,' he said, releasing a tight breath. 'I was going to contact you in any case and suggest a trial reconciliation. He just gave me the means to make sure you agreed to it.'

Claire sat in stony silence, wondering whether to believe him or not. He had certainly taken his time about contacting her; she had heard nothing from him for years. But then she began to wonder if it had something to do with the death of his father. Could Antonio have an ulterior motive for chaining her to his side? Suspicion began to make her scalp prickle. No wonder he had looked at her with such fury in his gaze while she had been talking to Isaac, and when she had questioned him about whether his father's estate had been divided between his brother and himself. She was starting to think Antonio would do anything rather than divide up his assets—even if it meant reconciling with his runaway wife.

'You have been on my mind a lot over the years, Claire,' he said into the silence. 'When this offer to come to Australia came up I decided it was a perfect opportunity to see if anything could be salvaged from what was left of our relationship. You had not pressed for a divorce, so I felt there was a chance you might still have feelings for me.'

'Well, you were wrong,' Claire said, tossing her napkin to one side and glaring at him as her anger towards him raced with red-hot speed through her veins. 'I feel nothing for you.'

He held her caustic look without flinching. 'That is not true, *cara*. You feel a lot of things for me. Anger and hate to name just two of them.'

'And that's not enough to send you and your blackmailed bride scheme packing?' she asked, with vitriol sharpening her voice to dagger points.

'Not until I know for sure there is no hope,' he said, with an intransigent set to his features. 'And the only way to find out is to start straight away —from tonight.'

Claire felt her eyes flare in panic. 'You can't mean for me to spend the night with you? Not yet. I'm not ready. It's too soon.'

He gave her an imperious smile, like someone who knew the hand they were about to spread out on the table was going to be a royal flush. 'You want to pull out of our deal?' he asked, reaching for his mobile. 'I can call Frank and tell him the police will be there in half an hour to pick up your brother and press charges on him.'

Claire clenched her hands beneath the table again. 'No, please,' she choked. 'Don't do that... I...I'll stay with you...'

His dark eyes travelled over her face for a pulsing moment. 'I will not force myself on you, Claire,' he said.

'You surely do not expect me to act so boorishly towards you, do you?'

She compressed her lips, waiting a beat or two before she released them. 'I'm not sure what to think…' she confessed. 'We're practically strangers now…'

'Even strangers can become friends,' he said. 'If nothing else, would that not be a good outcome of this three-month arrangement?'

Her eyes were wary as they met his. 'I can't imagine us exchanging Christmas cards and newsy e-mails, Antonio. Besides, we come from completely different worlds. I honestly don't know what I was thinking, getting involved with you in the first place.'

'Then why not tell me about your world?' he said. 'You hardly ever mentioned your family when we were together. You did not even want them to come to our wedding, though I offered to pay for their flights. I have never even seen a photograph of any one of them.'

Claire felt a tide of colour creep into her cheeks. 'They are my family, and I love them,' she said, knowing she sounded far too defensive. 'They're not perfect—far from it—but things have not been easy for any of them. My mother in particular.'

'What is she like?' he asked. 'You told me so little about her in the past.'

She tucked a corkscrew of curls behind her left ear, wondering where to begin. 'She's had a hard life. She lost her mother when she was in her early teens, and I guess because she felt so rudderless got pregnant at sixteen. Like a lot of other girls left holding the baby, she looked for love in all the wrong places, with each subsequent relationship producing a child but no reliable father. As the eldest and the only girl I kind of slipped into a pseudo-parenting role from an early age. My brother Callum is doing OK now, after a bit of a wild time in his teens, but it's Isaac I worry about. He's a little impulsive at times. He acts before he thinks.'

'He is young, and will eventually grow out of it if he is pointed in the right direction,' Antonio said. 'Frank Guthrie will be a good mentor for him. It sounds like your brother needs a strong male influence.'

Claire lifted her eyes back to his. 'Where did you meet this Frank guy?' she asked. 'I don't recall you mentioning him in the past.'

'I operated on his brother Jack about eighteen months ago,' he said. 'He was involved in a head-on collision just outside of Rome. There was a lot of facial damage. We had to put plates and screws in his forehead and cheeks, and rebuild both of his eye sockets. He was lucky to survive. No one thought he would come through, and certainly not without heavy scarring or disfigurement. I got to know Frank, who had flown over to be with him. He spent a lot of time at the hospital, so we often had a coffee and a chat after my ward rounds.'

'It must be very rewarding, seeing people recover from something like that,' she said. 'Your parents...I mean your mother...must be very proud of you.'

He gave her a wry half-smile. 'My father made it very clear when I first announced I was going to study medicine that he would have preferred me to take up the reins of his business. And my mother complained for years about the long hours I work. But I have always wanted to be a surgeon for as long as I can remember.'

Claire picked up her soda water again. 'How is your mother coping after your father's death?' she asked.

A shadow passed through his gaze as it met hers. 'She is doing as well as can be expected under the circumstances,' he said.

Claire was even more certain now that his father's death had everything to do with Antonio contacting her about this trial reconciliation. There would be certain expectations of him as the firstborn son of a wealthy businessman. An heir would be required. But he could hardly provide one whilst still legally married to his estranged wife.

A divorce between them had the potential to be messy, and no doubt very public. In their haste to marry close to six years ago, when Claire had announced her pregnancy, there had been no time for drawing up a prenuptial agreement. Antonio could not be unaware of how the family laws in Australia worked. She would be entitled to a considerable share of his wealth, including that which he had just inherited upon the death of his father, even though they had been living apart for so long.

She toyed with the edge of the tablecloth, struggling to keep her expression shuttered in case he saw how confused she was. It would be different if she still loved him. She would take him back without hesitation. But her love for him had died the day she had seen him in Daniela Garza's arms.

Or had it?

Claire looked at his face, her heart giving an unco-ordinated skip as her gaze came into contact with his coal-black eyes. She had been aware of a disturbing undercurrent the whole time they had been together this evening. Every time her eyes met his she felt the zap of attraction—unwilling, almost resentful, but no less unmistakable, and it definitely wasn't one-way. Her body recognised him as her pleasure-giver. She had not known such pleasure before or since, and while she imagined in her most tortured moments he had experienced physical ecstasy with many other women, she was more than aware of his ongoing desire for her. She could see it in his eyes, in the way they locked on hers for a second or two longer than necessary. She had felt it in the way his fingers had wrapped around hers in that possessive way of his, their warmth seeping into the coldness of hers. She could only imagine what would happen if he should kiss her at some point. Her lips could almost sense the gentle but firm pressure of his, and her tongue snaked out to try and remove the sensation. She didn't want to remind herself of all she had felt in his arms. She had locked away those memories. They were too painful to recollect.

They were far too dangerous to revisit.

'Have you finished playing with your meal?' Antonio asked.

Claire put down the fork she had been using to move around the seafood risotto she had been vainly trying to push past her lips. 'I guess I'm not as hungry as I thought I was,' she said, her shoulders going down on a sigh.

He took out his wallet and, signalling the waiter, placed his credit card on the table in anticipation of the bill. 'I will give you a night of reprieve, Claire,' he said. 'Go home and get a good night's sleep. If you give me a spare key to your flat I will send someone over tomorrow to shift your things to my suite at the hotel.

Do not worry about your lease or the rent for the next three months. I will see to that. All you need concern yourself with is stepping back into your role as my wife.'

He made it sound so simple, Claire thought as she drove back to her flat a short time later. All she had to do was pack a bag or two and slip back into his life as if she had never been away.

Even more worrying—how many nights would pass before he expected her to slip between the sheets of his bed?

CHAPTER SIX

THE salon was fully booked the following day, and it seemed as if every single client of Claire's had seen the press item documenting her reunion with Antonio Marcolini. All were intent on expressing their congratulations and best wishes. She smiled her way through each and every effusive comment, hoping no one would see through the fragile façade she'd put up.

Claire had refrained from telling Rebecca, her friend and employer, the finer details of her reconciliation with Antonio. How could she tell her closest friend that her estranged husband had more or less blackmailed her back into his life for the next three months?

But Rebecca must have sensed something in Claire's demeanour, and, cocking her head on one side, gave her a penetrating look. 'Claire, are you sure you're doing the right thing?' she asked. 'I mean, according to the papers he's only here for a limited time. What happens when he leaves at the end of August? Is he expecting you to go back to Italy with him?'

Claire bit her lip as she turned to fill the kettle in the small kitchen at the back of the salon. 'We haven't got around to discussing those sorts of details,' she said. 'We're taking it one day at a time, to see how things work out between us.'

Rebecca folded her arms, giving Claire a cynical look. 'So at any point he could just say *Forget it, it's over, I want a divorce.* Aren't any alarms bells ringing in your head?'

Claire puffed out a sigh. 'Look, I know it sounds a bit shaky, but he…*we* both feel it's worth a try. As he said, we were on his territory last time, and emotions were running high when we parted—or at least mine were. This way we can see if there is anything left to rebuild what we had before…before…things went wrong…'

Rebecca gave Claire's nearest arm a squeeze. 'If you need some time off to sort things out, just tell me,' she said. 'I can get Kathleen to come and fill in for you. She's been asking for the occasional day now her son's at preschool. You wouldn't be putting me out—not at all.'

'Thanks, Bex,' Claire said, with an attempt at a convincing smile. 'I'll see how it goes for now.'

Not long after her last client had left the salon door opened, and Claire looked up to see Antonio come in. She felt the ricochet of her reaction ripple its way through her as her eyes met his. Her stomach felt light and fluttery, her heart began to race, and her breathing intervals shortened.

Conscious of Rebecca's speculative look from the behind the reception desk, Claire was uncertain whether to greet him with a kiss or not. For five years she had thought of his kisses—those barely-there nibbles that had made her spine loosen, or the slow, drugging movement of his lips on hers that was a prelude to a drawn-out sensual feast, or the sexy sweep and thrust of his tongue, or the fast-paced pressure of his mouth grinding against hers as desire raced out of control.

No one had kissed her since him, Claire realised with a little jolt. She couldn't even bear the thought of anyone else claiming her lips. It didn't seem right, somehow, and not just because technically she was still married to him.

She looked up into his face, her heart giving a little kick against her breastbone when his gaze dropped to her mouth.

He slowly bent down and brushed his lips against hers, a light touchdown that made her lips instantly hungry for more. She opened her eyes to find his were half closed in a broodingly sexy manner, his focus still trained on her mouth. She moistened her dry lips with the tip of her tongue, her heart going like a piston in her chest as his mouth came back down.

It was a firmer kiss this time, purposeful, and with just the right amount of passion to awaken every nerve of awareness in Claire's body. Lightning bolts of feeling shot through her, tightly curled ribbons of need unfurling deep inside her, making her realise how desperately she still wanted him.

'Ahem…' Rebecca's discreet but diplomatic reminder that they were not alone came just as Claire had started to wind her arms around Antonio's neck.

She stepped out of his hold with a rush of colour. 'Sorry, Bex, I forgot to introduce you,' she said. 'Antonio, this is Rebecca Collins. Bex, this is Antonio Marcolini…my…er…husband.'

Claire watched as Antonio took Rebecca's hand with a smile that would have melted stone. It clearly went a long way to melting any cynical animosity Rebecca had felt previously, for she smiled back widely, congratulating him on coming to claim Claire.

'I'm so happy for you both,' she said, just short of gushing. 'I hope it all works out brilliantly for you. I've told Claire if she needs time off to spend with you, then that's fine. I have back-up. She needs a holiday in any case. She works far too hard as it is.'

Antonio drew Claire closer with one of his arms about her waist. 'I am looking forward to spending some downtime with her once the first rush of my lecture tour is over,' he said. 'I thought we might go on a second honeymoon in a few weeks' time, to somewhere warm and tropical and totally private.'

Claire fixed a smile on her face, her body already on fire at the thought of spending tonight with him in his hotel suite, let alone days and nights at a time in a tropical paradise.

There hadn't been time for a proper honeymoon the first time around. Claire had been suffering with not just morning sickness but all-day sickness, and Antonio had been sitting his final exams. Looking back, she wondered how they had lasted the year even without the tragedy of losing their baby girl. It seemed from the start everything had been pitted against them. Although in time Antonio had seemed to look forward to having their child, Claire had still felt his gradual pulling away from her. His increasing aloofness had made her overly demanding and clingy, which had achieved nothing but to drive him even further away. When she'd failed to produce a live heir he had let her go with barely a protest. That was what hurt the most. He hadn't fought for her. She had secretly hoped he would follow her back to Australia, demanding she come back to him, somehow circumventing the obstacles she had put in his way, but he had not.

Until now.

Antonio led Claire outside a few minutes later, to where she had parked her car. '*This* is your car?' he asked, frowning at her.

Claire lifted her chin. 'It gets me from A to B,' she said, adding silently, *Mostly*.

She could tell he was angry, but he seemed to be working hard to control it. 'Claire, if you have been having trouble making ends meet why did you not contact me?' he asked with a brooding frown.

She shifted her eyes from his. 'I didn't want your money,' she said. 'I just wanted to get on with my life.'

No, Antonio thought with a bitter twist of his insides. She hadn't wanted *his* money, but she had thought nothing of taking his mother's. If it took him every day of the three months he was here he would find out what she had done with it.

He gave her car—and that was using the word loosely—another scathing look. She clearly hadn't been spending up big in that department. In fact, there was no indication from what he had seen so far that she lived anything but a low-key life. She owned no real estate, either private or commercial, and her work at the salon was permanent, not casual. She dressed well, but if there was anything new and crafted by a high street designer in her wardrobe he had yet to see it. The black dress she had worn the evening before he had recognised as one he had bought for her in Paris. But then someone as naturally beautiful as Claire did not need the trappings of *haute couture* to showcase her assets. He had seen her in nothing but her creamy skin and he could hardly wait to do so again.

'I forbid you to drive this heap of rust,' he said, taking her keys from her hand before she could stop him.

She glared at him. 'Give me my keys!'

He pocketed them and, capturing her outstretched hand, led her back down the street. 'I will have someone move it later,' he said. 'And I will have a new car delivered to the hotel for you tomorrow.'

She trotted alongside him, tugging at his hold, but his fingers tightened. 'I don't want a new car,' she said. 'I don't want anything from you.'

He shot her a trenchant look as he turned her round to face him. 'If I want to buy my wife a new car, I will. For God's sake, Claire, you are driving around in a death trap. Does it even have airbags?'

She pulled her mouth tight. 'No, but—'

He swore viciously and continued striding towards his own car, parked in a side street. 'I suppose you have done it deliberately?' he said, using his remote to unlock the upmarket vehicle.

'What the hell is that supposed to mean?' she asked.

His eyes lasered hers. 'Do you have any idea of what the press would make of you driving around in that coffin on wheels? For God's sake, Claire, I am here to teach other surgeons how to repair the sort of damage people get from being drivers and passengers in unworthy road vehicles such as yours.'

'It's not an unworthy vehicle,' she said. 'It passed its registration inspection last year.'

He clicked the remote control device once they got to his car. 'How?' he asked with an indolent curl of his lip. 'Did you bribe the mechanic by offering *him* a service?'

The blue in her eyes burned like the centre of a flame as they warred with his. 'Only someone with your disgusting moral track record would think something like that,' she bit back furiously.

He held the passenger door open for her. 'I am not going to discuss this any further,' he said. 'You are not going to be driving it any more and that is final.'

Claire waited until he was behind the wheel before she spoke through tight lips. 'If you think by buying me a flash new car it will get me back into your bed, then you are not only wasting a heck of a lot of money but your time as well.'

He sent her a challenging look. 'I could get you into the back seat right now, Claire, and have you writhing beneath me within seconds.'

Claire felt her face fire up, and a traitorous pulse began deep and low in her belly. 'You would have to knock me out first,' she said with a derisive scowl.

He laughed and gunned the engine. 'I am looking forward to making you eat every one of those words, *tesoro mio*.' He thrust the car into gear. 'Every single one of them.'

Claire sat with a mutinous set to her mouth, but inside her stomach was quivering at the thought of becoming intimate with him again. When he looked at her in that smouldering way she felt as if she was going to burst into flames. Heat coursed through her. She was annoyed with herself for being so weak. What sort of wanton woman was she, to be allowing herself to fall all over again for his lethally attractive charm? Hadn't she learned her lesson by now? He was using her to keep her hands off his money. He thought far more of his inheritance than he did of her. He didn't care one iota for her. He never had. What other proof did she need? Hadn't she always known it in her heart? As much as she had longed for him to love her, she knew it was not going to happen. Not then, and not now.

Not ever.

After a few minutes of nudging his way through the clogged city streets, Antonio pulled into the parking bay of the hotel. One of the attendants opened Claire's door, while the valet parking attendant took Antonio's place behind the wheel.

Antonio took Claire's hand and led her inside the hotel to the bank of lifts. He didn't speak on the ride up to his penthouse suite, but Claire was aware of the undercurrent of tension building between them. She could feel it in his fingers where they were curled around hers, the warmth and the sensual strength searing into her flesh like a brand.

He swiped his security card and held the door of his suite open for her, waiting until she had moved past him before he closed it with a click that made her nerves jump.

'Relax, Claire,' he said, reaching up to loosen his tie. 'I am not going to throw you to the floor and ravish you, even though I am tempted.'

Claire chewed at her lip and watched as he shrugged off his jacket, his broad chest and lean, narrow hips making her want to press herself against him and feel every hard plane of his body.

He laid his jacket over the back of one of the sofas. 'Your things were brought over from your flat earlier today,' he informed her. 'One of the housemaids has placed them in the wardrobe in my bedroom.'

Claire looked at him with eyes wide with alarm. '*Your* bedroom?' she asked. 'You mean you expect me to share your bed…like…' she gulped before she could stop herself '…straight away?'

He gave her a bland look. 'Is that going to be a problem for you?'

She let out her breath in a gust of outrage. 'Of *course* it's a problem!'

'It is a big bed, Claire,' he said. 'I am sure I will hardly notice you are there.'

'Thanks,' she said with a resentful glare. 'That makes me feel as if I should just cover up all the mirrors right now, in case they shatter to pieces if I so much as happen to glance into them.'

His dark eyes glinted with amusement as he closed the distance between them. He pushed up her chin to lock gazes with her. 'You are searching for compliments, *si*?' he asked. 'Then I will give you one.' He brought his mouth down to hers, his lips moving against hers in a leisurely fashion, exploring, tasting and teasing.

Claire couldn't hold back her response when his tongue stroked the seam of her mouth for entry; she opened her lips on a sigh, her body sagging against his as he pulled her into his hardness. His tongue explored her thoroughly, reacquainting himself with every contour of her mouth, leaving her breathless with need when he finally lifted his mouth from hers.

'Now,' he said, with that same glint of amusement darkening his eyes, 'do you feel beautiful and desirable again?'

Claire looked into his eyes and felt her resolve slip even further away. Her mouth was still tingling all over from the sensual assault of his, her heart-rate so hectic she could feel it pumping against her breastbone.

She was unable to move out of his embrace, her body locked against the rock-hard wall of his, the unmistakable probe of his erection sending her senses into overdrive.

She lowered her eyes to look at his mouth, her belly giving a little flip of excitement when she saw his tongue move out to sweep over his lips, as if he was preparing to kiss her again.

She drew in a breath as his head came down, a soft whimper escaping from her lips just before his mouth sealed hers. The pressure was light at first, but within moments it subtly increased, his tongue going in search of hers, taking the kiss to a whole new level of sensuality as his groin pulsed against hers with growing need. She could feel the rigid outline of his erection, the length of him so familiar it felt like coming home. She rubbed herself against him, relishing in the feel of him, the way he groaned deep and low in the back of his throat as his hands cupped her bottom to bring her even closer.

His kiss became even more fervent, and her response was just as fiery as their tongues duelled and danced with each other. Her breasts felt achingly alive, tense and tingling with the need to feel his hands and mouth on them.

His hands moved from her bottom to slide up under her top, his palms deliciously warm as they skated over her quivering flesh. He unhooked her bra and she let out a breath of pure pleasure when his hands cupped the weight of her breasts, his thumbs pressing against the tight buds of her nipples.

He lifted his mouth from hers and brought it to her naked breast, that first moist stroke of his tongue evoking a sharp cry of delight from Claire's throat. He suckled on her then, softly at first, his teeth scraping gently, before drawing on her with hot, wet need. The raspy skin of his jaw was like fine sandpaper over her silky skin, but it only made her need for him all the more unbearable. She writhed impatiently against him, her body telling him what she was too proud to admit out loud. Desire flowed like a torrid flame, licking along her veins, igniting her passion to fever-pitch, making her breath come in short sharp gasps as his hands moved down between their pressed bodies and cupped the swollen heat of her feminine mound. Even though two layers of fabric separated his hand from her, Claire nearly exploded with need. He stroked her through her clothes, slowly, tantalisingly, until she was arching her back, desperate for more.

'You want me, *cara*?' he asked as he brought his mouth within a breath of hers.

Claire couldn't speak, and whimpered instead, her teeth nipping at his full bottom lip in tiny, needy bites.

He smiled against her lips. 'I want to hear you say it, *mia moglie poco passionale*—my passionate little wife. Tell me you want me.'

'I want you,' she said without hesitation this time. 'Oh, God, I want you.'

The light of victory shone in his eyes, but instead of bringing his mouth back down to hers he released her and, turning his back, strode casually across the room to the mini bar. 'Would you like a drink?' he asked over one shoulder.

Claire stared at him speechlessly, her arms crossing to cover her naked breasts, her heart feeling as if it had slipped from its rightful position in her chest. He couldn't have orchestrated a more devastating way to demonstrate how weak she was where he was concerned. Kissing her into submission only to walk away as if the erotic interlude had had no effect on him at all.

'No, thank you,' she said, and with fumbling fingers tried to do up the buttons on her blouse. But her vision suddenly blurred, making the simple task impossible.

'Here,' he said, coming back over to where she was standing. 'Let me.'

Claire's heart thumped harder and harder as his steady fingers slowly but surely refastened each tiny button, her mouth trembling slightly when he got to the last ones, between her breasts. She dragged in a breath, the expansion of her chest bringing his fingers into contact with the slight swell of her right breast.

His eyes meshed with hers for a pulsing moment. 'It *will* happen, Claire,' he said, sliding his hand to the nape of her neck in a light but possessive touch that sent another shiver of sensation racing up and down her spine.

She swallowed again, not sure she would be wise to contradict him, given what had almost happened moments earlier.

It will happen.

Oh, how those words set her senses on full alert! She could almost feel him plunging inside her, the length and breadth of him filling her, stretching her, making her shatter into a thousand pieces of ecstasy. How many times in the past had she been his willing slave to sensuality? One look, one touch, and she had been on fire for him, her body feeling as if it was going to explode with pleasure as soon as he nudged her trembling thighs apart.

'But then,' he said, moving his hand to trail his fingers down the curve of her cheek, 'sex was never a problem for us, was it?'

Claire compressed her lips, her eyes skittering away from his. She was not going to fall for that again, to openly admit her need of him just so he could gloat over the sensual power he still had over her. He wanted to grind her pride in the dust, but she was going to do everything possible to thwart him. It would take every gram of self-control, but she would do it.

His hands settled on her waist, bringing her close to his body. 'We were good together, were we not, Claire?' he said. 'Better than good, in fact. Do you remember the way you used to relieve me with your mouth?'

Claire's whole body quivered in response to his erotic reminder of how she had pleasured him in the past. She had been an eager learner and he had taught her well. She had done things with him she had never thought she would do with anyone. The carnal delights he had given and taken still made her blush. His eyes had always scorched her with one look—just as they were doing now.

'Don't do this…' she said, struggling to keep her voice even.

He gave her a guileless look. 'Don't do what?' he asked.

She moistened her lips, hardly realising she was doing it until she saw his eyes drop to her mouth and follow the movement. 'You're trying to destroy my pride. I know you are. It's all a game to you, isn't it? Making me admit I still want you just so you can leave me dangling.'

'I am entitled to recall our most intimate moments together, am I not?' he asked. 'I can hardly erase them from my memory. I just have to look at that soft full mouth of yours and I want to unzip my trousers and push your head down.'

'Stop it,' Claire said, putting her hands over her ears to try to block the incendiary temptation of his words. 'Stop doing this. It won't work.'

He pulled her hands away from her head and brought her up close, pelvis to pelvis, his hot, hard need against her soft, moist ache. 'What are you frightened of, *cara*?' he asked. 'That you might discover you do not hate me as much as you claim? Is that it?'

Claire refused to answer. She clamped her lips together, glaring at him, her heart pounding with a combination of anger and out-of-control desire.

'The fact is you do *not* hate me, Claire,' he said. 'You just hate the fact that you still want me.'

'I do hate you,' she said, wrenching out of his hold. 'You slept with that—'

'Damn you, Claire.' He cut her off. 'How many times do I have to tell you there was nothing going on between us?'

'Your mother told me,' Claire said, putting up her chin at a combative height. 'She told me you had been lovers for a long time and were planning to marry, but that I had ruined everything by falling pregnant. She said you would never have married me if it hadn't been for my accidental pregnancy. She said that Daniela had been unofficially engaged to you for years.'

Antonio felt every muscle in his body tense. He had broken things off with Daniela a couple of months before he had met Claire. Daniela had taken it well, having come to the conclusion herself that their relationship had run its course. She had seemed to understand his need to focus on his career. Yes, they had once or twice laughed off their respective parents' none-too-subtle hints that a marriage between them would be more than agreeable, but he had never been in love with her, and as far as he could tell she had not been in love with him.

The afternoon Claire had seen them together had been as innocent as it had been coincidental. He had been having a quiet non-alcoholic drink with a colleague, both being on call, when Daniela had turned up, having seen him from the street outside. His colleague had left after a half an hour and Daniela had stayed on, expressing her concern over how Antonio was coping with the strain at home. It had been no secret he and Claire were having problems after the stillbirth of their baby. The last couple of months had been particularly dire, with Claire's shifting moods. He had done everything in his power to help her, but it had seemed nothing he said or did was what she wanted. She had oscillated between bouts of hysterical accusation and cold stonewalling, shutting him out for days on end.

Daniela had been supportive, and, knowing him as she had for so many years, had understood his private and internal way of processing the pain of his grief in a way Claire had not been ready or willing or even able to understand.

When Claire had come across them in the foyer, hugging as they had said goodbye, she had immediately misconstrued the situation. Daniela had made a diplomatic exit, but Claire had drawn him into a blazing row out on the street, which had been interrupted by an emergency page from the hospital, where one of his patients had begun bleeding post-operatively. By the time he'd got home the following morning, after more than twelve hours of horrendously difficult surgery, Claire had packed her bags and left.

As to what Claire had just intimated about his mother, there was no way Antonio could verify that now. As far as he knew Claire had demanded a large sum of money from his mother, and once his mother had written the cheque Claire had taken it and left the country. He had arrived at the airport just as her plane had taken off. The anger he had felt at that moment had carried him through the weeks and months ahead, and it had been refuelled every time Claire had refused to answer her phone or respond to his e-mails. Pride had prevented him chasing after her, even though not a day had gone past when he hadn't considered it. He knew it had been stubborn of him, leaving it so long, but he was not the type to beg and plead. He had finally accepted she had moved on with her life, and he had more or less done the same. It had only been when she had started the divorce process that he'd realised what was at stake—and not just his money. They had unfinished business between them, and this time around it was going to be done on his terms and his terms only.

'Perhaps you misunderstood what my mother said,' Antonio offered. 'Her English is not quite as good as it could be.'

Claire's blue-green eyes sent him a caustic glare. 'I know what I heard, Antonio,' she said. 'And besides, your mother speaks perfectly understandable English. Why don't you ask her what she said to me that night? Go on—call her up and ask her. Put the phone on speaker. She can hardly deny it with me standing right here listening to every word.'

Antonio sent splayed fingers through his hair again, releasing a breath that caught on something deep inside his chest on its exit. 'I do not wish to upset my mother right now,' he said. 'She has not been well since the death of my father.'

She gave a disdainful snort. 'You Italians really know how to stick together, don't you? I know blood is thicker than water and all that, but Marcolini blood is like concrete.'

'It is not about taking sides, Claire,' he said. 'The issues that brought about our estrangement need to be addressed by you and me personally. I do not want to drag in a jury on either side to complicate things any further.'

'What about Daniela?' she asked. 'Have you spoken to *her* lately?'

'No, not lately,' he answered. 'She got married about a year ago, to a friend of one of my cousins who lives in Tuscany. She is expecting a baby; I am not sure how far along she is now—pretty close to delivery, I should think. I have not spoken to her since my father's funeral.'

Claire tried to ignore the deep stab of pain she felt every time she heard of someone else's pregnancy. She seriously wondered sometimes if she would ever be able to feel happy and hopeful for another mother-to-be. How could they be so complacent, so assured of a healthy delivery? Did they really think a good diet and moderate exercise would guarantee them a live baby? She had done all that and more, and look where it had led. She had gone home empty-handed, shattered, shell-shocked. Every tiny bootie and delicately embroidered and knitted outfit had screamed at her from the walls of the beautifully decorated nursery she had seen to herself: where is the baby for all this stuff?

There had been no baby.

Instead there had been a tiny urn of ashes which Claire had carried all the way back to Australia, to give her daughter the interment she felt her baby deserved.

'If my mother somehow misinformed you about my relationship with Daniela, I am deeply sorry,' Antonio's voice broke through her painful thoughts. 'The only excuse I can offer on her behalf is that she was probably concerned our marriage was on the rocks, and thought it would help you to come to some sort of decision over whether or not to continue with it.'

Claire hugged her arms close to her chest, her teeth savaging her bottom lip as she thought about Antonio's explanation for his mother's behaviour. It sounded reasonable on the surface. Their marriage certainly hadn't been a rose-strewn pathway, and they hadn't exactly been able to hide it from his family. Claire cringed at the thought of how often she had sniped at Antonio in their presence towards the end.

Doubts started to creep up and tap her on the shoulder with ghost-like fingertips. What if she had got it totally wrong? What if what she had seen that day had been exactly as Antonio had tried to explain it at the time?

Claire's own insecurities, which had plagued her

from the beginning of their hasty marriage, had made her vulnerable to suggestion. She had immediately jumped to the conclusion Daniela and Antonio had enjoyed a mid-afternoon tryst in the hotel that day. She had not for a moment considered any other explanation. But then maybe she hadn't wanted to? Claire thought in retrospect. Maybe Antonio was right about his mother. Rosina Marcolini had been concerned her daughter-in-law was miserably unhappy, and had been so from the start. She had probably assumed Claire was no longer in love with her son, so had given her a way out of the situation. Rosina had obviously told her son it was Claire who had asked her for money, not she who had offered it, but proving it now was going to be difficult—unless she could challenge his mother face to face.

Claire looked up at Antonio. 'When you didn't come home at all that night I assumed you were with Daniela.'

He frowned at her. 'But don't you remember I got an emergency page to go back to Theatre?' he asked. 'When I saw how bad things were with the patient I asked one of the theatre staff to call you to let you know I was going to be late. She tried several times to call, but each time it was engaged or went through to the message service. In the end I told her to give up, as I did not want to be distracted from the difficult case I was working on. The patient was in a bad way and I needed to focus.'

Claire bit her lip again. She had been so angry and upset she had turned her mobile off and left the landline off the hook. It had only been after Antonio's mother had dropped by and had that short but pointed conversation with her that she'd decided to pack her bags and leave.

Antonio came closer and took her hands in his. 'I

got home at six in the morning to find you had gone,' he said. 'I lost valuable time thinking you had gone to stay with one of the friends you had made from the Italian class you attended. By the time it was a reasonable hour to call one of them to check you had already boarded the plane. I got to the airport just in time to see it take off. I was angry—angrier than I had ever been in my life. I could not jump on the next plane to follow you as I had patients booked in for weeks ahead. So I decided to let you go. I thought perhaps some time with your family would help you. God knows nothing I did ever seemed to work. But when you consistently refused to take my calls I realised it was over. I thought it was best you got on with your life while I got on with mine.'

Claire lowered her gaze to look at their linked hands. There were no guarantees on their current relationship. He had not made any promise of extending their reconciliation beyond the three-month period. She knew he desired her, but then he was in a foreign country without a mistress at the ready. What better way to fill in the time than with his wayward wife—the one who had got away, so to speak? A man had his pride, after all, and Antonio Marcolini had more than his fair share of it. Claire had done the unthinkable to him. Walking out on him without once begging to be taken back.

This set-up he had orchestrated might very well be a cleverly planned plot to serve his own ends. He knew a divorce would be costly; he no doubt realised he had to keep her sweet as so much was now at stake—his father's millions, for one thing. A temporary affair would stall divorce proceedings for several months.

Long enough for him to find some way out of handing her millions of dollars in settlement.

She pulled her hands out of his. 'I think you did the right thing in leaving me to get on with my life,' she said. 'We both needed time to regroup.'

'Perhaps,' he said, looking at her for a long moment. 'But five years is a long time, Claire.'

'Yes, and I needed every minute of it,' she said, with another lift of her chin.

His mouth thinned. 'How many lovers have there been? How many men have come and gone from your bed?'

Her eyes flashed at him. 'I hardly see what business that is of yours.'

He reached for her hands again, tethering her to him with long, strong fingers. 'How soon did you replace me?' he asked, holding her gaze with the searing heat of his.

She tried to get out of his hold but his fingers tightened. 'Why do you want to know?' she asked, glaring up at him.

His jaw tensed, a nerve at the side of his mouth pulsing like a miniature hammer beneath his skin. 'Have you had casual affairs, or something more permanent?' he asked.

'There's been no one permanent,' Claire said, tugging at his hold again. 'Now, let me go. You're hurting me.'

He looked down at his hands around her wrists and loosened his hold without releasing her. His thumbs began a slow stroke of the underside of each wrist, making her spine lose its rigid stance. Claire closed her eyes against the tide of longing that flowed through her. His body was so close she could feel its tempting warmth. The urge to feel his hardness against her again was suddenly irresistible, and she tilted towards him before she could stop herself. It was a betraying movement, but she was beyond caring. For some reason his demonstration of jealousy had stirred her, making her wonder if he felt something for her after all. It had been so long since she had felt anything but this aching sadness and emptiness inside. Would it be so very wrong to succumb to a moment of madness? Making love with Antonio would make her forget everything but the magic of his touch, how he could make her feel, how he could make her body explode time and time again with passion. It was what she wanted; it was what they both wanted.

Antonio held her from him. 'No, Claire,' he said firmly. 'Not like this. Not in anger and recrimination.'

Claire looked up at him in confusion. 'I thought your whole idea was to get me back into your bed as quickly as possible?'

His expression left her little to go on. 'I am not denying my intention of resuming a physical relationship with you, Claire, but if I were to follow through on your invitation just now I am sure you would hate me all the more tomorrow.'

She raised her brows at him. 'Scruples, Antonio?' she asked. 'Well, well, well—who would have thought?'

He stepped away from her, his mouth once again pulled into a taut line. 'If you would like to shower and change, we have a charity function to attend this evening,' he said. 'The dress is formal. You have just under an hour to get ready.'

Claire frowned. 'You expect me to come with you?'

His look was ruthlessly determined. 'I expect you to be by my side, as any other loving wife would want to be. No public displays of temper, Claire, do you understand?'

She pressed her lips together in resentment, not trusting herself to speak.

'I said, do you understand?' he repeated, pinning her with his coal-black gaze.

She lifted her chin. 'I hate you, Antonio,' she said. 'Just keep thinking about that tonight, while I am hanging off your arm and smiling at the cameras like a mindless puppet. I *hate* you.'

He shrugged off her vitriol as smoothly as he did his jacket; he hooked his finger under the collar of it, his eyes still holding hers. 'Just think how much more you are going to hate me when I have you begging in my arms, *tesoro mio*.'

Claire swung away from him, anger propelling her towards the bathroom. She slammed the door behind her, but even under the stinging spray of the shower she could still feel the promise of his words lighting a fire beneath her skin. Every surface the water touched reminded her of how he had touched her in the past: her breasts, her stomach, her lower back and thighs, and that secret place where the tight pearl of her womanhood was swollen with longing for the friction of his body. She hated herself for still wanting him. It made her feel like a lovesick fool who had no better sense than to get her fingers burned twice. That she had been a lovesick fool the first time round was more than obvious to her now. Antonio had probably been laughing at her gaucheness from the start of their affair. She had been a novelty to him—a girl from the bush, an innocent and naïve girl who had been knocked off her feet by his sophisticated charm.

Claire turned off the shower and reached for a towel with grim determination. She would show him just how much she had grown up and wised up over the last five years. He might think he could cajole her back into his bed as easily as he had the first time, but this time around she was not going down without a fight.

CHAPTER SEVEN

ANTONIO was flicking through some documents on his lap when Claire came out of the bedroom, close to forty-five minutes later. She felt his gaze run over her, taking in her upswept hair, the perfection of her understated make-up, and the flow and cling of her evening dress, in a fuchsia-pink that highlighted the creamy texture of her skin and the blue-green of her eyes.

He put his papers to one side and rose to his feet. 'You look very beautiful, Claire,' he said. 'But you have forgotten something.'

Claire frowned and put a hand up to check both her earrings were in place. 'What?'

He picked up her left hand. 'You are not wearing your wedding and engagement rings.'

Claire felt her stomach go hollow. 'That's because I no longer have them,' she said, not quite able to hold his look.

He brought up her chin with the end of his finger, locking his gaze with hers. 'You sold them?' he asked, with a glint of anger lighting his eyes from behind.

'No,' she said, running her tongue across her lipgloss. 'They were stolen not long after I got back from Italy.

My flat was broken into one day when I was at work. My rings were the only things they got away with. The police said the burglars had probably been disturbed by someone and took what they could and bolted.'

His finger stayed on her chin for several heart-chugging seconds. 'Were the rings covered by an insurance policy?'

'No…I couldn't afford it, and—'

'That is not true, though—is it, Claire?' he said, with that same glitter of simmering anger in his diamond-hard gaze. 'You could well afford it, but you chose to spend the money my mother gave you on other things.'

Pride made Claire's back stiffen. 'So what if I did?' she said. 'What are you going to do about it?'

His hand dropped from her face as if he didn't trust himself to touch her. 'We will be late if we do not leave now,' he said tersely.

Claire followed him out to the lifts. The smooth ride down was conducted in a crackling silence. As soon as the doors swished open he put a hand at her elbow and escorted her to a waiting limousine. She pasted a stiff smile on her face for the benefit of the hotel staff and their driver, but inside she was seething. Acting the role of his reconciled wife was going to be much more difficult than she had first imagined. There was so much bitterness between them, so much ingrained distrust and resentment.

Antonio leaned forward to close the panel separating them from the driver. As he sat back one of his thighs brushed Claire's, and she automatically shifted along the seat.

He gave her a smouldering look that sent a shiver

down her spine. 'You did not find my touch so repulsive an hour or so ago, Claire.'

She sent him a haughty glare in the vain hope of disguising her reaction to him. 'I must have been out of my mind. I can think of nothing I want less than to sleep with you again.'

He smiled a lazy smile as he moved closer, until he was touching her thigh to thigh, his hand capturing one of hers. Claire flinched at his touch, and he frowned and looked down at the faint bracelet of fingertip bruises he had unknowingly branded her with earlier.

His smile disappeared and a heavy frown furrowed his brow. He picked up her other hand and turned it over, ever so gently. '*I* did this?' he asked in a husky tone as he met her eyes.

Claire swallowed tightly. His touch was achingly gentle now, his fingers like feathers brushing over the barely-there bruises. His eyes were so dark, intensely so, as if the pupils had completely taken over his irises. Her heart began to thud, in an irregular rhythm that made her chest feel constrained.

'It's n-nothing…' she said with a slight wobble in her voice. 'I probably knocked myself against something…'

He was still frowning as he looked back at her wrists. 'Forgive me,' he said, low and deep. 'I had forgotten how delicately you are made.'

Claire held her breath as he lifted each of her wrists in turn to his mouth, the soft salve of his kisses stirring her far more deeply than the words of his apology could ever do. His lips were a butterfly movement against her sensitive skin, a teasing of the senses that made her realise how terribly unguarded she was around him.

Her heart shifted inside her chest like a tiny insect's wings, beating inside the narrow neck of a bottle.

His eyes came back to hers, his fingers loose as they held her hands within his. 'Do they hurt?' he asked in a gravel-like tone.

She shook her head, still not trusting herself to speak. She felt choked-up, emotion piling right to the back of her throat in a great thick wad of feeling she couldn't swallow down, no matter how hard she tried. Her eyes began to burn with the effort of keeping back tears, and she had to blink rapidly a couple of times to stave them off. This was the Antonio she had fallen so deeply in love with all those years ago. How was she supposed to resist him when he sabotaged her resolve not with force but with tenderness?

Antonio released her hands with a sigh. 'We have to sort this out, Claire. I know you think I have engineered this to my advantage, but we both have to be absolutely sure about where this ends up.'

Claire could already guess where it was going to end up. She was halfway there already: back in love with him, back in his arms, dreaming of a happy ever after when there were no guarantees she would ever have a nibble at the happiness cherry again. She could almost taste the hard pip of reality in her mouth. He didn't love her. He had never loved her the way she longed to be loved—the way her mother had never been loved, even after three desperate tries to get it right. Was Claire facing the same agonising destiny? A life of frustrated hopes? Girlhood dreams turned to dust as thick as that lining the roads of the Outback where she had grown up?

The limousine purred to a halt outside a convention

center, and within moments the press were there to capture the moment when Antonio Marcolini and his wife, newly reconciled, were to exit the vehicle.

Claire thought she had hidden her discomfiture well as she got out of the car with Antonio by her side, but somehow, in the blur of activity and the surging press of the crowd, she met his gaze for the briefest of moments and realised she had not fooled him—not even for a second.

He offered her his arm and she looped hers through it with a smile that tugged painfully at her face. 'Do we have to do this?' she whispered with a rueful grimace. 'Everyone is looking at us.'

He picked up a tendril of her curly hair and secured it behind her ear. 'We have to, *cara*,' he said, meshing his gaze with hers. 'We need to show ourselves in public as much as possible.'

Claire drew in a scratchy breath and, straightening her shoulders, walked stride by stride with him into the convention center. But for some reason she felt sure he hadn't been referring to the glamorous evening ahead, but more about the night that was to follow...

The table they were led to was at the front of the ballroom, where the other guests were already seated. Each person stood and greeted Antonio formally, before turning to greet her with smiles of speculative interest.

Drinks were served as soon as they sat down, and Claire sipped unenthusiastically at a glass of white wine as convivial conversation was bandied back and forth around her. She smiled in all the right places, even said one or two things that contributed to the general atmosphere of friendliness, but still she felt out on a ledge. She didn't belong here—not amongst his colleagues, not amongst his friends. She had never belonged, and somehow sitting here, with the lively chatter going on around her, it brought it home to her with brutal force. Even listening with one ear to one of the women at the table describing the latest antics of her toddler son felt like a knife going through Claire's chest. Her mind filled with those awful moments after her baby had been delivered, the terrible silence, the hushed whispers, the agonised looks, the shocking realisation that all was not as it was supposed to be.

'Claire?'

Claire suddenly realised Antonio was addressing her, his eyes dark as the suit he was wearing as they meshed with hers. 'Would you like to dance?'

She sent the tip of her tongue out to sweep away yet another layer of lipgloss. 'Dance?'

He smiled—Claire supposed for the benefit of those around them, watching on indulgently. 'Yes,' he said. 'You were very good at it, I seem to remember.'

Claire lowered her gaze to stare at the contents of her glass. 'I haven't danced for ages…'

'It does not matter,' he said, taking her by the hand and gently pulling her to her feet. 'This number is a slow waltz. All you have to do is shuffle your feet in time with mine.'

She had a lot more to do than shuffling her feet, but after a while Claire relaxed into it, relishing the feel of Antonio's arms around her as he led her in a dance that was a slow as it was sensual. Each step seemed to remind her of how well-matched their bodies were, the union of male and female, the naturalness of it, the ebb and flow of moving in time with each other as if they had been programmed to respond in such a way. His thigh pushed hers backwards, hers moved his forwards, and then they moved together in a twirl that sent the skirt of her long dress out in an arc of vivid pink.

'See?' Antonio said, smiling down at her as he led her into another smooth glide across the floor. 'It is like riding a bike, *si*? You never forget the moves.'

Claire could feel her body responding to his closeness. His pelvis was hard against hers, with not even the space for a silk handkerchief to pass between their bodies. She felt the stirring of his body, the intimate surge of his male flesh that made her ache for his possession all over again. She tried to convince herself it was just a physical thing: he was a virile man, she was a young healthy woman, and the chemistry that had brought them together in the first place had been reawakened. Sex with an ex or an estranged partner was commonplace. The familiarity of the relationship and yet that intriguing element of forbidden fruit made resisting the urge to reconnect in the most elemental way possible sometimes unstoppable. She could feel that temptation now; it was like a pulse deep in her body, a rhythm of longing that would not go away no matter how much she tried to ignore it.

'You are starting to tense up on me,' Antonio said. He ran his hands down the length of her spine as the number came to an end, and an even slower, more poignant one took its place. 'Relax, *cara*, there are people watching us.'

How could she possibly relax with his hands resting in the sensitive dip of her spine like that? Claire felt as if every nerve was set on super-vigilance, waiting for the stroke and glide of his next touch. Her belly quivered and her skin lifted in a fine layer of goosebumps as she met his dark, intense gaze.

'I'm not used to such big crowds these days,' she said. 'I haven't been out for ages. Compared to you, I live a very quiet life.'

He rested his chin on the top of her head as they moved in time with the music. 'There is nothing wrong with living a quiet life,' he said. 'I sometimes wish mine was a little less fast paced.'

Claire breathed in the scent of him as they circled the floor again. It felt so right to be in his arms, as if she belonged there and nowhere else. The trouble was she wasn't sure how long she was likely to be there. He seemed very intent on sorting out the train wreck of their previous relationship, but his motives for doing so were highly suspect.

It was so hard to tell what Antonio was thinking, let alone feeling. He had always been so good at keeping his cards close to his chest. She, on the other hand, wore her heart on her sleeve and had done so to her own detriment. She had made herself far too vulnerable to him from the outset, and now she felt as if she was doing it all again. He knew he had her in the palm of his hand. He knew she would not do anything that would jeopardise her brother's well-being. That was his trump card, and she was too cowardly to call his bluff, even though she dearly wanted to.

But even without the threat of Isaac facing the authorities, Claire suspected she was in too deep now to extricate herself. She couldn't quite get rid of the nagging fear she had got her wires twisted over his alleged affair with Daniela Garza. If so, she had ruined both of their lives by impulsively leaving him. The very thing she lectured her brother Isaac on time and time again was the very thing she most hated in herself: acting before thinking. How would she ever be able to forgive herself if she had got it wrong?

Antonio skilfully turned her out of the way of another couple on the dance floor, his arms protective around her. 'You look pensive, *cara*,' he said. 'Is something troubling you?'

Claire worried her bottom lip with her teeth, finally re-leasing it to look up at him. 'If you weren't having an affair with Daniela, why didn't you share the same bed as me after we lost the baby? You never came to me—not once.'

His expression tightened, as if pulled by invisible strings underneath his skin. 'That was because I thought it better to leave you to rest for the first couple of days, without me taking calls from the hospital late at night and disturbing you. It was clear after a while that you did not want me to rejoin you. You seemed to want to blame me for everything. I was damned no matter what I did, or what I said or did not say.'

Claire felt the dark cavern of her grief threatening to open up and swallow her all over again. He was right— she *had* blamed him for distancing himself. But hadn't she done the very same thing? She had been so lost, so shell-shocked at her loss, it had made it so hard for her to reach out to him for comfort. She had wanted to, many times, but when he'd taken to sleeping in the spare room, or staying overnight at the hospital, she had lain in the sparse loneliness of the bed they had shared and cried until her eyes had been almost permanently red-rimmed and swollen.

She had never seen him shed a single tear for their tiny daughter. She knew people grieved in different ways, but Antonio and his family had all seemed much the same in dealing with the stillbirth. They'd simply got on with their lives as if nothing had happened. Apart from the first day after Claire came out of hospital the baby had never been mentioned—or at least not in Claire's presence. There had been a brief christening in the hospital, but there had been no funeral. Antonio's parents had not thought it appropriate, and in the abyss of her grief she had gone along with their decision because she had not wanted to face the heartbreaking drama of seeing a tiny coffin carried into a church. It had only been later, once she was back in Australia, that she had felt ready to give her daughter a special place to rest.

The music had stopped, and Claire grasped at the chance to visit the ladies' room to restore some sort of order to her emotions. She mumbled something to Antonio about needing to touch up her lipgloss and, conscious of his gaze following her every step of the way, made her way to the exit.

She locked herself inside one of the cubicles in the ladies' room and took several deep breaths, her throat tight and her eyes aching with the bitter tears of regret.

For all this time she had relished placing the blame for the collapse of their relationship on Antonio. She had so firmly believed he had betrayed her. But in hindsight she could see how immature and foolish she had been right from the start. She had been no more ready for marriage than he had; she had been too young—not just in years, but in terms of worldly experience. He at least had had the maturity to accept responsibility for the pregnancy, and he hadn't even insulted her by insisting on a paternity test, as so many other men might have done. How had she not realised that until now? He might not have loved her, but at least he hadn't deserted her. He had stood by her as much as his demanding career had allowed.

Was it really fair to blame him for not being there for the delivery? He was a surgeon, for God's sake. He had the responsibility of other people's lives in his hands every single day. She hadn't even asked him why he hadn't made it in time. She had jumped to the conclusion that he had deliberately avoided being there because he hadn't wanted the baby in the first place—which was yet another hasty assumption she had made. He might have been initially taken aback by the news of her pregnancy, but as the weeks and months had gone on he had done his best to come with her to all of her prenatal appointments and check-ups. She had even caught him several times viewing the ultrasound DVD they had been given of the baby, wriggling its tiny limbs in her womb. He had bought a baby name book for her, and had sat with his hand gently resting on her belly as they looked through it together.

Claire had never realised how physically ill remorse could make one feel. It was like a burning pain deep inside, gnawing at her, each savage twinge a sickening reminder of how she had thrown away her one chance at happiness. Yes, they had experienced a tragedy, one that neither of them would ever be able to recover from fully, but this was the only opportunity she would get to do something to heal the disappointment and hurt of the past. It was optimistic, and perhaps a little unrealistic, to hope that Antonio would fall in love with her this time around, but she had three months to show him her love was big enough for both of them.

When she came out a few minutes later, Antonio rose from the table to hold out her chair for her, his dark eyes moving over her features like a searchlight, a small frown bringing his brows together. 'Is everything all right, *cara*?' he asked. 'You were away for so long I was about to send someone in to find you.'

Claire shifted her gaze and sat down. 'I'm fine; there was a bit of a queue, that's all.'

The woman seated opposite leaned forward to speak to her. 'I read about the reconciliation with your husband in the paper this morning. I am sure you'll be very happy this time around. I've been married to John for thirty-five years this September. We've had our ups and downs, but that's what marriage is all about—give and take and lots and lots of love.'

Claire stretched her mouth into a smile. 'Thank you. I am sure there will be plenty of hard work ahead, but, as you say, that is what marriage is all about.'

'My husband is a plastic surgeon as well,' the woman who had introduced herself as Janine Brian continued. 'He's very impressed with some of the new techniques Antonio is demonstrating. You must be very proud of him. He has brought new life and hope to so many people all over the world.'

'Yes…yes, I am,' Claire said, glancing at Antonio, who was now deep in conversation with one of the other guests at the table. She felt her breath lock in her throat as he turned his head to look at her, as if he had sensed her gaze resting on him.

She couldn't stop staring at him; it was like seeing him for the very first time. She marvelled at how handsome he looked in formal dress, how his tuxedo brought out the darkness of his eyes and hair, and how the stark whiteness of his dress shirt highlighted the deep olive tone of his skin. His mouth was tilted at a sexy angle, as if he knew exactly where her thoughts were leading. How could he possibly know how much she wanted to explore every inch of his body as she had done so often in the past? Could he see the hunger in her eyes? Could he sense it in the way her body was tense and on edge, her hands restless and fidgety, her legs crossing and uncrossing under the table? Desire was an unruly force in her body. She felt it running like a hot river of fire beneath her skin, searing her, branding her inside and out with the scorching promise of his possession.

'You two are just so romantic,' Janine said with an indulgent smile. 'Look at them, John.' She elbowed her husband in the ribs. 'Aren't they the most-in-love couple you've ever seen?'

Claire felt a blush steal over her cheeks as Antonio came back to sit beside her. He placed an arm around her shoulders, drawing her close. 'I was a fool to let her get away the first time,' he said. 'It will not be happening again, I can assure you.'

'Well, you know what they say: there's nothing better than making up in the bedroom,' Janine said. 'That's how we got our three kids, wasn't it, darling?'

'Janine…' John Brian frowned.

'What did I say?' Janine frowned back.

'It is OK, John,' Antonio said, giving Claire's shoulder a little squeeze. 'Claire and I cannot expect everyone to be tiptoeing around the subject of children for the rest of our lives.'

Janine Brian's face fell. 'Oh, dear…I completely forgot. John did tell me about… Oh, how awfully insensitive you must think me. I'm so, *so* sorry.'

Claire gave the distressed woman a reassuring smile, even though it stretched at her mouth uncomfortably. 'Please don't be upset or embarrassed,' she said. 'Each day has become a little easier.'

The conversation was thankfully steered in another direction when the waiter appeared with the meals for their table. Claire forced herself to eat as if nothing was wrong for Janine's sake, but later she would barely recall what it was she had eaten.

After the meals were cleared away, Antonio was introduced by the chairman of the charity. Claire watched as he moved up to the lectern, which had been set up with a large screen and data projector. After thanking the chairman and board members, Antonio spoke of the work he carried out in reconstructive surgery under the auspices of FACE. He showed pictures of some of the faces he had worked on, including several from Third World countries, which the charity had sponsored by bringing patients to Rome for surgery to be performed.

Claire looked at one of the young children he had worked on. The little girl, who was seven or eight, had been born with hyperteliorism, a congenital condition which presented as a broad face with wide, separated eyes and a flat nose. Fixing it required major cranial-facial reconstruction, with a team of three surgeons: a neurosurgeon, a facial maxillary surgeon and a plastic surgeon. In this case it had been Antonio. The team had operated for twelve hours to give the little girl a chance at a normal life, without shame or embarrassment over her unusual appearance. The before and after photographs were truly amazing. So too were the happy smiles of the child's parents and the little girl herself.

Once Antonio had finished his presentation he took some questions from the floor before returning to the table to thunderous applause.

The band began to play again and Antonio reached for Claire's hand. 'Let's have one more dance before we go home,' he suggested.

Claire moved into his arms without demur, her own arms going around his neck as his went around her back, holding her in an intimate embrace that perfectly matched the slow rhythm of the ballad being played.

'I thought you handled Janine Brian's little slip very graciously,' Antonio commented after a moment or two.

She looked up at him with a pained expression. 'Thank you,' she said. 'But you're right in saying we can't expect people to avoid the subject of babies all the time. I have friends with little ones, and I have taught myself to enjoy visiting them, even babysitting them without envy.'

He looked down at her for a beat or two. 'That is very brave of you, Claire.'

She gave him another little grimace before she lowered her gaze to stare at his bow tie. 'Not really… There are days when it's very hard…you know…thinking about her…'

Antonio felt the bone-grinding ache of grief work its way through him; it often caught him off guard—more lately than ever. Being with Claire made him realise how much losing a child affected both parents, for years if not for ever. The mother bore the brunt of it, having carried the baby in her womb, not to mention having the disruption of her hormones during and after the delivery. But the father felt loss too, even if it wasn't always as obvious as the mother's. Certainly the father hadn't carried the child, but that didn't mean he didn't feel the devastation of having failed as a first-time father.

Antonio had grown up with an understanding of the traditional role of husband and father as being there to protect his wife and children. He might have gone into marriage a little ahead of schedule, due to the circumstances of Claire's accidental pregnancy, but when their baby had died it had cut at the very heart of him. He had felt so helpless, swamped with grief, but unable to express it for the mammoth weight of guilt that had come down on top of it.

He wondered if Claire knew how much he blamed himself, how he agonised over the 'what if' questions that plagued him in the dark hours of the night. He still had nightmares about arriving at the delivery suite to find her holding their stillborn baby in her arms. A part of him had shut down at that point, and try as he might he had never been able to turn it back on. He felt as if he had fallen into a deep, dark and silent well of despair, locked in a cycle of grief and guilt that to this day he carried like an ill-fitting harness upon his shoulders.

The music changed tempo, and even though she didn't say a word Antonio felt Claire's reluctance to stay on the dance floor with him. He could feel it in her body, the way she stiffened when he drew her close. Whether she was fighting him or fighting herself was something he had not yet decided. But then he had the rest of the night to do so, and do so he would.

He felt a rush of blood in his groin at the thought of sinking into her slick warmth again. The tight cocoon of her body had delighted him like no other. It made his skin come alive with sensation thinking about her hands skating over him the way they'd used to, tentatively, shyly, and then boldly once her confidence with him had grown. The feel of her soft mouth sucking on him that first time had been unbelievable. He had felt as if the top of his head was going to come off, so powerful had been his response. He wanted to feel it all again, every single bit of it—her touch, her taste, the tightness of her that made his body tingle for hours afterwards.

'Time to go home?' he asked as he linked his fingers with hers.

Her cheeks developed a hint of a blush. 'Yes…if you like…' she said, her gaze falling away from his.

Antonio led her back to the table, from where, after a few words of farewell to the other guests, he escorted her out to the waiting limousine. It would take them back to his hotel, where she would have to share his bed in his arms or spend the night alone on the sofa.

It would be interesting to see which she chose.

CHAPTER EIGHT

IT WAS a mostly silent trip on the way back to the hotel.

Antonio looked at Claire several times on the way, but each time she had her gaze averted, and her fingers were restless as they toyed with the catch of her evening purse.

'Do I unsettle you so much, *cara*?' he asked, as the car purred to a smooth halt outside the hotel.

She turned her gaze on him, a shadow of uncertainty shining in their ocean-blue and green depths. 'A little, I guess,' she confessed as he helped her out of the car.

Antonio led her into the hotel, his hand at her elbow, his stride matching her shorter one. He pressed the call button for the lift, and as he waited for it to come turned to look at her. 'I told you, Claire, we will not resume a physical relationship until we are both ready. I am not going to force myself on you. You can be absolutely sure of that.'

She rolled her lips together as she lifted and then dropped her gaze again. 'I'm not sure what I want… that's the problem…I feel confused right now…'

He tipped up her chin with the end of his index

finger. 'I want you,' he said. 'I think you know that. That is something that has not changed in the last five years.'

'But is this right…what we're doing?' she asked, the tip of her tongue sneaking out to sweep over her lips. 'It seems to me we're back together for all the wrong reasons.'

The lift came to a stop at Antonio's penthouse floor, and he held the doors open with his forearm for Claire to move past.

He swiped his key and led her into the suite, closing the door behind him. 'We have a past, Claire,' he said, securing her gaze with his. 'We have to deal with it one way or the other.'

She bit her bottom lip, her throat moving up and down over a little swallow. 'But is this the right way?' she asked. 'What if we make more problems than we've got now?'

'Like what?' he asked, pulling at his bow tie.

She gnawed at her lip again, releasing it after a second or two to say, 'I don't know…it's just I don't want any misunderstandings to develop between us.'

He tossed his bow tie and his jacket on the nearest sofa. 'The whole point of this exercise is to see if what we started out with is still there, hidden under the sediment of our separation,' he said heavily. 'I do not want to go through the messy process of a divorce only to take the same unresolved issues to another relationship.'

Claire felt her heart clamp with pain. 'So this arrangement you've orchestrated between us is basically an experiment?' she asked, frowning at him.

He held her look for a moment before he blew out a sigh. 'I want to get on with my life, Claire. You need to get on with yours. Neither of us can do that until we work through this.'

She pulled herself upright and faced him squarely. 'So what you're really saying is you need to have a three-month affair with me to see if there is anything worth picking over before you move on to the next woman you want to get involved with. Is that it?'

He gave her a brooding look. 'No, that is not it at all.'

Claire felt as if her hopes and dreams were about to be shattered all over again. Would she ever be anything more than a fill-in for him? Was it too much to ask him to care something for her?

Her rising despair made her voice come out sharper than she had intended. 'Then what the hell is it about, Antonio? I just don't know what you want from me.'

He took her gently but firmly by the shoulders, his dark eyes almost black as they pinned hers. 'I think deep down you know exactly what I want from you, cara,' he said and, swooping down, captured her mouth with the searing warmth of his.

Claire had no hope of resisting such a potently passionate kiss. Flames of need licked along her veins, sending her heart-rate soaring as Antonio's tongue probed for entry, the hot searching heat of him making her whimper in response. She could feel her lips swelling under the pressure of his, her body melting into his embrace as he pulled her closer. She felt the erotic ridge of his erection against her—a heady reminder of all the passion they had shared in the past and how earth-shattering it had been.

His mouth continued its sensual assault on her senses as his hands went from her waist to her lower back, the gentle pressure of his hand against her lumbar region bringing her right up against the hard probe of his arousal. Her belly quivered at that intimate contact, her legs becoming unsteady as a raging tide of desire flooded her being.

His kiss became deeper and more insistent, and Claire responded with the same ardour. She took his full bottom lip in her teeth, gently tugging, then sucking, and then sweeping her tongue over it in a caress that brought a groan from deep inside him.

His hands pressed her even harder against him; even the barrier of his clothes did not lessen the sensation of feeling the potent length of him so close to the heart of her need. Her body was already preparing itself; she could feel the slick moistness gathering between her thighs, her breasts tight and aching for the feel of his mouth and hands.

His kiss became even more urgent as she moulded herself against him, his tongue more insistent as it mated with hers.

She reached between them and shaped him with her fingers, her mouth still locked under the scorching heat of his. He made another guttural sound of pleasure, and she increased the pace of her stroking, up and down, glorying in the licence to touch him, to feel him pulsing with such intense longing for her.

He dragged his mouth from hers, looking down at her with eyes so dark with arousal they looked bottomless. 'Are you sure this is what you want, *cara*?' he asked in a husky tone. 'We do not have to continue with this if you do not feel ready.'

Claire moistened her passion-swollen lips as she held his gaze. 'I'm not sure about anything,' she said. 'I can't seem to put two thoughts together in my head when you are around.'

His wry smile was intoxicatingly sexy. 'Then maybe we should not think, but instead concentrate on feeling,' he said, moving his hand to the zipper at the back of her dress and slowly but surely sliding it down until the satin pooled at her feet.

Claire felt her breath catch as his dark gaze ran over her, taking in her naked breasts, the flat plane of her stomach, the slight flare of her hips and the tiny black lace panties she was wearing.

Her breathing almost stopped altogether when he trailed a fingertip down between her breasts, circling each one before he bent his head and took each tightly budded nipple in his mouth. It was torture and pleasure rolled into one, and the sparks of fiery need shooting up and down her spine at the rasp of his tongue made every rational thought fly out of her head.

He lifted his head and, locking his gaze on hers, sent his fingertip down to the cave of her belly button, and then lower, tracing over the cleft of her body through the lace that shielded her. 'Take them off,' he commanded in a toe-curling tone.

Claire kicked off her heels and peeled off the tiny lace garment, her heart kicking in excitement as he began to undress. Becoming impatient, she helped him with the buttons of his shirt, stopping every now and again to press a hot, moist kiss to his chest, then lower and lower, until she came to the waistband of his trousers.

He shrugged his shirt off and stood with his thighs slightly apart as she undid his belt, pulling it through the loops until it joined her dress on the floor.

She heard him draw in a breath as her fingers pulled down his zipper, and then she felt him jerk in awareness when she peeled back his underwear to touch him skin on skin.

He was like satin-covered steel under her fingertips, and so aroused he was seeping with moisture. She blotted it with her fingertip and then, lifting her eyes to his, brought her finger up to her mouth and sucked on it.

'*Dio*, you are driving me crazy,' he growled, as he heeled himself out of his shoes, his trousers and underwear landing in the same heap as his belt and her dress.

Claire drew in an uneven breath as he walked her backwards towards the bed, his hands on her hips, the heated trajectory of his body setting her alight all over again. She could smell his arousal, the hint of salt and musk that was as intoxicating as the notes of citrus she could pick up from his aftershave.

'Tell me to stop, Claire, otherwise I will not be able to,' he groaned as his mouth brushed against hers.

She linked her arms around his neck, pushing her pelvis against his. 'I don't want you to stop,' she said in a breathless whisper. 'It's been such a long time…'

'You are right about that,' he said as he eased her down on the bed, his eyes devouring her all over again before he joined her. 'It has been far, far too long.'

Claire shivered as his long, strong legs brushed against her smooth ones. The arrant maleness of him had always made her heart race with excitement. The hardness of his body against her dewy softness made her feel light-headed with anticipation. She arched her spine in invitation, aching for him to pin her body with his, to drive her towards the paradise she craved.

'Not so fast, *cara*,' he said, stroking his hands over her belly, thrillingly close to where she pulsed for him.

'You know how it was between us before. It was always much more intense when we took our time.'

Claire sucked in a breath as he bent his head to her breasts, his mouth and tongue inciting her passion to an almost unbearable level. The hot trail of his kisses continued down her sternum to the tiny dish of her belly button, and then over the faint stretchmarks on both of her hips, before moving to the throbbing core of her body. Her breath skidded to a halt in her chest as his fingers gently separated her, the tender, honeyed flesh opening to his stroking touch. He set a slow but tantalising rhythm, each movement bringing her closer and closer to the release she could feel building and building inside her. Then she was there: her back lifting off the bed, her senses soaring out of control, as wave after wave of ecstasy smashed over her, rolling her, tossing and tumbling her, until she felt totally boneless, limp with satiation.

Claire reached for him, her fingers circling his hardness before she slithered down to brush her mouth against him. She felt a shudder go through him when she traced him with the point of her tongue. He was still in control—but only just. His breathing was choppy and uneven, each and every one of his muscles taut with tension as she drew him into her mouth, tasting him, tantalising him with the butterfly caress of her tongue.

'No,' Antonio growled suddenly, and pulled her away. 'I want to come inside you. I have waited so long for this.'

Claire felt her insides tremble with excitement as his body settled over her, one of his thighs nudging hers apart, his weight propped up on his elbows as he drove into her with a deep groan of satisfaction. She felt the skin of his back and shoulders lift in a shiver as her body grabbed at him hungrily, the rocking motion he began setting her alight all over again. Electrifying sensations shot through her with each stroke and smooth glide of his body in hers. She felt the tremors begin deep inside her, the ripples of reaction rolling through her as he increased his pace, each deep thrust taking her higher and higher. She felt as if her body imploded, so forceful was the release he evoked. It rocketed through her like a torpedo, making every nerve hum and sing with sensation.

Antonio's breathing quickened, his thrusts now so deep and so purposeful Claire could feel the exact moment his control finally slipped. With a deep groan he burst inside her, his body shuddering against hers as pleasure coursed through him, her tight body milking him until he collapsed in satisfaction above her.

She kept stroking his back, her fingers dancing over his muscled form, hoping the magical spell of sensuality would not be broken too quickly.

Antonio was right: this was the part they had always got right. It was the other details of their relationship they had tripped over: the involvement of relatives, the demands of his career and the loss of her independence, not to mention the vicissitudes of life, which in their case had been particularly cruel.

Antonio shifted his weight to look down at her. 'It has not changed, has it, *cara*?' he said, brushing a damp curl back from her forehead. 'Although perhaps I am wrong about that; it *has* changed—if anything it has got better.'

Claire trembled under his touch, her body acutely aware of his, still lying encased moistly in hers. 'What if it's not enough, Antonio? Physical attraction will eventually burn itself out. Then what will be left?'

His eyes were dark as pitch as they held hers. 'It has not burned out yet, in spite of our five-year hiatus. As soon as I saw you again I realised it. I wanted you back in my bed no matter what it took to get you there.'

'This can't go anywhere,' she said, dropping her gaze from his in case he saw too much of what she was feeling. She was like a toy he had decided to play with for a limited time. She had to keep reminding herself this was not for ever. He was only here for three months.

'It can go where we want it to,' he said. 'For as long as we want it to.'

Claire felt a prickle of alarm run over her bare flesh as she brought her gaze back to his. 'I'm not sure what you're saying,' she said, flicking her tongue out over her lips. 'This is temporary…isn't it?'

His gaze went to her mouth, halted, and then lifted back to hers. 'Are you on the pill?' he asked.

Something dark and fast scuttled inside Claire's chest, making her feel breathless, as if the faceless creature of fear had buried itself in the chambers of her heart. 'Um…no…' she said, unable to hold his gaze.

He nudged her chin up with the point of his finger, his dark eyes drilling into hers. 'No?'

She rolled her lips together, trying to think where she was in her cycle. 'I'm not on it at the moment…' she said, grimacing slightly.

He kept his gaze steady on hers for several heart-chugging seconds. 'Do you think you are in a safe period?' he asked with an unreadable expression.

'Yes,' she said, even though she was not quite sure. It would be disastrous if she was to fall pregnant by him, setting off another heartbreaking cycle of waiting and hoping, and yet...

Oh, God, the thought of another chance at being a mother was so very tempting. Maybe this time it wouldn't end in tragedy, in spite of the information she had sought on the internet. She had learned that after a previous incident of placental abruption the chances of a second occurring was between ten and seventeen percent. The statistics stated that whereas one out of one hundred and fifty deliveries cited a case of placental separation, the severe form, where foetal death occurred, was only one in five hundred.

It was all a matter of chance...

'Are you sure?' Antonio asked, his gaze now darkened with intensity.

She nodded and eased herself away from him, hugging her knees to her chest to affect some measure of decency. 'But even if we had used a condom there's no guarantee it would have prevented a pregnancy,' she said. 'That's how it happened the last time, if you remember?'

'Yes, but only because you had not been taking the pill long enough for it to be effective,' he said.

Claire felt resentment rise up in her like a viper wanting to strike at its tormentor. 'So you're blaming me for what happened in the past, is that it? It was my fault for being so naïve in thinking I was covered when I wasn't? We would not have had to go through any of what we went through if I had taken the time to read the leaflet in the box? Is that what you are saying?'

A deep crevasse appeared between his brows. 'I did

not say that, Claire. An unplanned pregnancy can happen to anyone.'

She still felt herself bristling in spite of his response. 'Then what exactly *are* you saying?'

It seemed a long time before he answered. 'This is probably not the right time to bring up the subject of babies.'

Claire felt the faint hope she had secretly harboured in her chest deflate at his words. He was after a good time, not a long time. He was at a loose end in a foreign country. No wonder he had looked her up—hooked up with her in a blackmail bargain that would see him as the only winner at the end. He wanted no ties, no lasting consequences of their brief encounter. Just like last time he wanted a short, hot, full-on affair to compensate for the punishing hours he worked.

He also wanted revenge, she reminded herself. He wanted to have things on his terms this time. He would be the one to walk away, not her.

'I can't do this,' she said, springing off the bed to snatch up a bathrobe hanging on the back of the door. She thrust her arms through the sleeves and tied the waistband securely before she faced him again. 'I can't do casual, Antonio. I'm not built that way.'

'This is not casual, Claire,' he said, locking gazes with her. 'We are still married.'

She frowned at him, her heart fluttering in panic. 'What do you want from me?' she asked in a broken whisper.

'I want you, Claire,' he said with an intransigent look as he stepped towards her. 'This is not over. You know that. What happened in that bed just minutes ago proved it beyond any shadow of a doubt.'

Claire tried to back away from him but came up against the wall. 'What happened in that bed was a stupid mistake on my part,' she said, flattening her spine against the cold hard surface behind her. 'I got carried away with the dancing and the wine. I wasn't in my right mind. You should have known that.'

He lifted one brow in a perfect arc of derision. 'It seems to me it is only my fault when you do something you later regret,' he said.

'You're trying to make me fall in love with you, aren't you?' she asked.

He came closer, his eyes meshing with hers. 'Is that your biggest worry, *cara*?' he asked as he trailed his index finger down the curve of her cheek, before tracing over her top lip in a nerve-tingling caress.

Claire's biggest worry was how she was going to prevent a repeat of what had just occurred between them. The sex had been mind-blowing and blissfully satisfying. Even now she could feel her body responding again to his nearness. It didn't help that she was totally naked beneath the bathrobe she was wearing. She could feel the way her breasts were pushing against the soft fabric, her nipples still swollen and sensitive from his mouth. She could feel the moistness of his essence between her thighs. She could even smell the fragrance of their coupling—an intoxicating reminder of how she had fallen apart in his arms and how easily it could happen again. She was hard-wired to respond to him. No one else could affect her the way he did. The intimacy they had shared had only intensified her longing. She could feel it building in her; it was like an on-off pulse deep inside.

She was acutely aware of how he was watching her,

with that dark, intelligent gaze of his, noting every nuance of her expression, every movement of her body as it stood so close to his.

He placed his hands either side of her head, on the wall behind her, not just trapping her with the brackets of his arms but with his eyes as well. 'Would falling in love with me be a problem?' he asked.

Claire ran the tip of her tongue over her lips, her chest rising and falling on an uneven breath as she looked into his deep dark gaze. 'It…it would only be a problem if it wasn't reciprocated.'

His eyes went to her mouth. 'If we fall in love then we will not need to go through a divorce,' he said, bringing his gaze back to hers. 'A good solution, *si*?'

She tightened her mouth. 'For you, maybe, but not for me,' she said. 'I'm not going to move back to Italy with you.'

He measured her with a cool, appraising look. 'You might not have a choice if you have conceived my child,' he said. 'I am not prepared to be separated by thousands of kilometres from my own flesh and blood.'

Claire felt her heart lurch, panic fluttering like startled wings inside her chest. 'If I have fallen pregnant there is no guarantee it will end in a live birth,' she said, trying to ignore the blade of pain that sliced through her at admitting it out loud. 'If you want to become a father you would be well advised to pick someone who is capable of doing the job properly.'

His eyes held hers for a tense moment before he dropped his hands from the wall. 'I am aware of the statistics, Claire,' he said. 'But with careful monitoring it may not happen again.'

'I am not prepared to risk it,' Claire said. 'If we are going to continue this farcical arrangement I want you to use protection. I will see my doctor tomorrow about arranging my own.'

Antonio watched as she pushed herself away from the wall, her arms around her middle like a shield, her eyes flashing resentment and pent-up anger against him.

He could still feel the tight clutch of her body around him, the way she had convulsed to receive every drop of his seed. He wanted her so badly it was a bone-deep ache inside him; it had never gone away, no matter how hard he had tried to ignore it. And she wanted him, even though she resented it and did her best to hide it. Her body betrayed her just as his had. And it would betray her again. Of that he was sure.

CHAPTER NINE

CLAIRE slipped past Antonio to the plush bathroom and closed the door firmly behind her. She considered locking it, but upon inspecting the device recognised it was one of those two-way models which could be unlocked from either side of the door—no doubt installed as a safety feature, in case a guest in the hotel slipped and fell in the bathroom. She realised the only lock she really needed was a lock on her heart, but as far as she knew no such item existed. She was as vulnerable to Antonio as she had ever been—maybe even more so now she had experienced such rapture again in his arms.

She stepped into the shower stall, hoping to wash away the tingling sensations Antonio's touch had activated, but if anything the fine needle spray of the shower only made it worse. Her whole body felt as if every nerve beneath her skin had risen to the surface. Every pore was swollen and excited at the anticipation of the stroke and glide of his hands, the commandeering of his mouth. She touched her breasts. They felt full and heavier than normal, and her nipples were still tightly budded, the brownish discs of her areolae aching all over again for the sweep and suck of his mouth.

Her hands went lower, over the flat plane of her belly and down to the cleft of her body where he had so recently been. She felt tender and swollen, still acutely sensitive, the intricate network of nerves still humming with the sensations Antonio had evoked.

She turned the water off and reached for a fluffy white towel. But even after she was dried off and smothered all over with the delicately fragrant body lotion provided, she felt the tumultuous need for fulfilment racing through her body.

The hotel suite was large, but it only contained one bed—and Claire knew she would be expected to share it with Antonio. Because of their history, she also knew there would be no demarcation line drawn down the middle of the mattress.

Antonio was a sprawler. She knew there would be no hope of avoiding a brush with a hair-roughened limb or two. It would be a form of torture, trying to ignore his presence. If it was anything like in the past he would reach for her, drawing her close to him, like two spoons in a drawer, his erection swelling against her until she opened her thighs to receive him as she had done so many times before.

Her mind began to race with erotic images of how he had taken her that way: the breathing of him against her ear as he plunged into her wetness, the pace of their lovemaking sped up by its primal nature, the explosion of feeling that would make her cry out and make him grunt and groan as each wave of ecstasy washed over them, leaving them spent, tossed up like flotsam on the shore.

Claire exchanged the towel for the bathrobe and, tying the belt securely around her waist, took a steadying breath and opened the door back into the suite.

Antonio was sitting with his ankles crossed, a glass of something amber-coloured in his hand. 'Can I get you a drink, Claire? You look as if you need something to help you relax.'

She gave him a brittle glance. 'The last thing I need is something that will skew my judgement,' she said. 'What I need is a good night's sleep—preferably alone.'

His mouth tilted at a dangerously sexy angle. 'There is only one bed, *tesoro mio*. We can fight over it, if you like, but I already know who will win.'

Claire knew too. That was why she wasn't even going to enter into the debate. She eyed the sofa. It looked long enough to accommodate her, and certainly comfortable enough. She would make do. She would *have* to make do—even if it meant twice-weekly trips to a physiotherapist to realign her neck and back as a result.

Antonio got to his feet in a single fluid movement. 'Do not even think about it, Claire,' he said, placing his drink down with a clink of glass against the marbled surface. 'Our reconciliation will not be taken seriously if the hotel cleaning staff come in each day and see we have not been sleeping in the same bed.'

Claire fisted her hands by her sides and glared at him. 'I don't want to sleep with you.'

He gave her an indolent smile. 'Sleeping is not the problem, though—is it, *cara*?' he asked. 'We could sleep in the same bed for weeks on end if we were anyone other than who we are. Our bodies recognise each other. That is the issue we have to address in sharing a bed: whether we are going to act on that recognition or try to ignore it. My guess is it will continue to prove impossible to ignore.'

I can ignore it, Claire decided—although with perhaps not quite the conviction she would have liked, given what had occurred less than an hour ago.

Antonio pulled back the covers on the bed. 'I will leave you to get settled,' he said. 'I am going to have a shower.'

She clutched the edges of the bathrobe tightly against her chest. 'Do you expect me to stay awake for you— to be ready to entertain you when you get back?' she snipped at him.

He smoothed the turned-back edges of the sheet before he faced her. 'I expect no such thing, *cara*,' he said. 'You are tired and quite clearly overwrought. Perhaps you are right. I should not have taken advantage of your generous response to my attentions. I thought we both wanted the same thing, but in hindsight perhaps I misjudged the situation. If so, I am sorry.'

Claire captured her bottom lip, chewing at it in agitation. He made it sound as if he had ravished her without her consent, when nothing had been further from the truth. She had practically ripped the clothes off his body in her haste to have him make love to her. She had been as out of control as he had, her need for him like an unstoppable force—a force she could still feel straining at the leash of common sense inside her, waiting for its moment to break free and wreak havoc all over again.

'It's not your fault…' The words slipped out in a breathless rush. 'I shouldn't have allowed things to go so far. I don't know why I did. I don't think it was the wine or the dancing…it was just…curiosity… I think…'

His brows arched upwards again. 'Curiosity?'

Her tongue darted over the surface of her lips, her gaze momentarily skittering away from his. 'I guess, like you, I wanted to know if it would be the same…you know…as it had been before…before things went wrong…'

He came closer and, using his finger, brought up her chin so her eyes met his once more. 'We cannot change what happened,' he said. 'Our past is always going to be there, whether we continue our association or not. We will both carry it with us wherever we go in the future, and whoever shares our future will have to learn to accept it as part of who we are.'

Her eyes misted over. 'Hold me, Antonio,' she whispered as her arms snaked around his middle. 'Hold me and make me forget.'

Antonio held her close, lowering his chin to the top of her silky head, breathing in the freshly showered flowery fragrance of her as his body stirred against her. He wanted her again, but he was conscious that this time her need for him was motivated by a desire for solace, not sensual fulfilment. He closed his eyes and listened to her breathing, feeling the slight rise and fall of her chest against his, every part of him aching to press her down on the bed and possess her all over again.

He'd had to rein in such impulses before. In the weeks following the loss of their baby he had thought the best way to help her heal would be to mesh his body with hers again—to bring it back to life, to start again, to reignite the passion that had flared so readily from the moment they had met. But she had been so cold, so chillingly angry, as if he had deliberately orchestrated the demise of their daughter. Her reaction had been like an IV line plugged into the bulging vein of his guilt, hydrating it, feeding it, until it had flowed through every pore of his body, poisoning him until he finally gave up.

Antonio stroked the back of her hair, the bounce of her curls against his fingers making the task of holding her at bay all the more difficult. She was crying softly, so softly he would not have known it except for feeling the dampness of her tears against his bare chest. He was used to tears. How many patients had fallen apart in his consulting rooms over the years? Time and time again he had handed them tissues and spoken the words and phrases he'd hoped would make the burden they faced a little easier to bear. And most times it had worked. But it hadn't worked with Claire. Not one word he had spoken had changed anything.

He knew his feelings were undergoing a subtle change, but he wasn't ready to examine them too closely. He had been trained to see things from a clinical perspective. He had seen for himself how often emotions got in the way, complicating the decision-making process. What he needed was a clear head to negotiate his way through the next few months.

Divorce was a dirty word just now. It had always been a dirty word in his family. His parents were of the old school, their religious beliefs insisting on marriage being 'until death do us part'. His father's will might easily have been remade in the years since Claire had left, but Salvatore had done nothing. Antonio had told himself it was a simple oversight—like a lot of people his father hadn't expected to die so soon—but he wondered if there had been more to it than that.

Antonio hadn't been particularly close to either of his

parents since late adolescence. His desire to be a surgeon had not been met with the greatest enthusiasm, and he had subsequently felt as if he had let them down in some way, by not living the life they had mapped out for him. He had been assured of their love growing up, and certainly they had done everything possible to support him during his long years of study, but the chasm that divided them seemed to get bigger as each year passed.

His father had only once spoken to him about Claire's desertion. Antonio had still been too raw from it all; he had resented the intrusion into his personal life, and after a heated exchange which had caused months of bitter stonewalling between them eventually his father had apologised and the subject had never been raised again. His mother too had remained tight-lipped. Over the last five years he could not recall a single time when she had mentioned Claire's name in his presence.

Looking back now, he realised he had not handled things well. He had allowed his anger and injured pride over Claire leaving him to blur his judgement. He had been so incensed by her accusation of him having an affair that he hadn't stopped to think why she had felt so deeply insecure, and what he had done or not done to add to those feelings. He had believed her to be looking for a way out of their relationship, and he had done nothing to stop her when she took the first exit.

Antonio put her from him with gentle hands. 'Go to bed, Claire,' he said. 'I will sleep on the sofa tonight.'

She looked up at him, her eyes still glistening and moist. 'I don't want to be alone right now,' she said, so softly he could barely hear it.

His hands tightened on her shoulders. 'Are you sure?'

She nodded, her teeth sinking into her bottom lip. 'Please, Antonio, don't leave me alone tonight. I just couldn't bear it.'

Antonio sighed and slid his hands down the length of her arms, his fingers encircling her wrists. 'You make it so hard to say no, Claire,' he said, looking down at the faint marks he had left on her tender skin. 'Everything about you makes it hard to say no.'

She placed her hands on his chest, looking up at him with luminous eyes. 'I want to forget about the past,' she said. 'You are the only person who can make me forget. Make me forget, Antonio.'

He brought his mouth down to hers in a kiss that was soft and achingly tender. The pressure of his lips on hers was light at first, gently exploring the contours of her mouth. He took his time, stroking her lips until they flowered open on a little sigh. His tongue danced just out of reach of hers, tantalising her, drawing her to him, challenging her to meet him in an explosive connection.

Claire could not resist the assault on her senses; her tongue darted into his mouth, found his and tangled with it boldly, while her lower body caught fire against the hard pressure of his holding her against him. She felt the swollen ridge of his erection through the thin barrier of the boxer shorts he had slipped on earlier. Her hand went down, cupping him through the satin, relishing the deep groan he gave as her fingers outlined his length. She felt his breathing quicken, and slowly but surely lowered the shorts until she was touching him skin on skin, her fingers circling him. Delighted with the way he was pulsing with longing against her, she began to slide her fingers up and down, slowly at first, knowing it would have him begging in seconds—and it did.

He growled against her passion-swollen mouth. 'Please, *cara*, do not torture me.'

She smiled against his lips—a sensual woman's smile, not a shy young girl's. 'You want me to go faster?' she asked huskily.

He nipped at her bottom lip once, twice, three times. 'I think you know what I want, *tesoro mio*. You seem to always know what I want.'

Claire left the bathrobe slip from her shoulders, her eyes watching his flare as he drank in the sight of her naked. His gaze felt like a brand on her flesh; each intimate place it rested felt hot and tingling. Her breasts swung freely as she pushed him back onto the bed, coming over him like a cat on all fours, pausing here and there to lick him, her belly quivering with desire as, each time her mouth came into contact with his flesh, he gave a little jerk of response. His hands bunched against the sheets as she came closer and closer to the hot, hard heat of him. She took her time, each movement drawn out to maximise his pleasure. A little kiss here, a little bite there, a sweep of her tongue on the sharp edge of his hip before she nipped at him with her teeth, each touch of her mouth making his back arch off the bed and a gasping groan came from his lips.

Claire had dreamt of this moment over the years. Alone in her bed, miserably unhappy and unfulfilled, she had dreamed of being with Antonio again, having him throbbing with need for her and only her, just as he was doing now. He was close to losing control. She could sense it in every taut muscle she touched with her hands or lips or tongue. But she still hadn't got to the *pièce de résistance* in her sensual repertoire.

She met his eyes; his were smoky, burning with expectation, totally focussed on her. 'If you want me to beg, then keep doing what you are doing,' he said between ragged breaths. 'But be warned, there will be consequences.'

She gave him a devil-may-care look as she moved down his body with a slithering action. 'I can hardly wait,' she breathed, and bent to the task at hand.

Claire sent her tongue over him first, in a light, cat-like lick that barely touched the satin of his strained flesh. But it was enough to arch his spine. She did it again, stronger this time, from the base to the moist tip, her tongue circling him before she took him in her mouth.

He shuddered at the first smooth suck, his hands going to her head, his fingers digging into her curls, as if to ride out the storm of feeling she was evoking.

Claire tasted his essence, drawing on him all the harder, delighting in the way she was affecting him. She could hear his breathing becoming increasingly rapid, the tension in his muscles like cords of steel as he flirted with the danger of finally letting go.

In the end Claire gave him no choice. She intensified her caresses. Even when he made a vain attempt to pull away she counteracted it, pushing his hand aside as she drew on him all the more vigorously. She heard him snatch in a harsh-sounding breath, his fingers almost painful at they held on to her hair for purchase. He exploded in three short sharp bursts, his body shuddering through it, his chest rising and falling, his face contorted with pleasure as the final waves washed through him.

Claire sat back, a little shocked at how wanton she had been, when only minutes before she had been insisting she was not going to share a bed with him. She had shared much more than a bed now, she realised. The act she had just engaged in was probably the most intimate of all between couples.

She could still remember the first time she had done it. She had been shy and hesitant, wondering if somehow it was wrong, but Antonio had coached her through it with patience, all the time holding back his passion until she had felt comfortable enough to complete the act. It had taken a few tries, but he hadn't seemed to mind. And besides, he had done the same to her—many times. The first time he had placed his mouth on the secret heart of her she had nearly leapt off the bed in reaction, so intense had been the feelings. But over time she had learned to relax into the caress of his lips and tongue, forgetting her shyness and simply enjoying his worship of her body demonstrated time and time again.

Antonio pushed her gently back down on the pillows, his ink-black eyes meshing with hers. 'I owe you,' he said.

Claire felt her belly quiver like unset custard. 'I feel like a hypocrite,' she confessed.

'Why is that?' he asked as he brushed his mouth over her right breast.

She pulled in a sharp breath as her nipple tightened. 'I told you I didn't want to sleep with you, but that is clearly not the case—given what just happened.'

'So, who is sleeping?' he asked, looking at her with a smouldering look.

She began to gnaw at her bottom lip again, her brow furrowing.

'Hey,' he said, stroking her lip with the tip of his index finger. 'Stop doing that. You will make yourself bleed.'

Claire ran her tongue over her lips and encountered his finger. The contact was so erotic she felt a tug deep inside her abdomen.

He was giving her that look—the look that meant she was not going to go to sleep tonight without experiencing the cataclysmic release he had planned for her in return for what she had done to him.

'Lie back,' he commanded deeply.

Claire shivered as she eased back down on the mattress. Her nakedness would barely even have registered in her consciousness if it hadn't been for his searing gaze, drinking all of her in. She saw the way his eyes focussed on her breasts, the way his gaze moved down over her belly to where the triangle of her womanhood was barely concealed by the tiny landing strip of dark, closely cropped curls. It was as close to a Brazilian wax as her pain centres had allowed on her last beauty salon visit, but now she wished she had gone the whole distance. She wanted to please him, to surprise him, to show him she was no longer an innocent girl from the Australian Outback, starstruck by his good looks and status. She was a woman now—a woman who knew what she wanted. And what she wanted was him.

If it was only going to be for three months then she would settle for that. She had dealt with loss before and survived. She had made the mistake of living in the past too long. It was well and truly time to move on, to live in the moment as so many of her peers did. They didn't worry about a few weeks of pleasure with a casual lover. They didn't agonise over whether or not they should sleep with a man they were seriously attracted to. They just did it and enjoyed every minute of it.

Claire's life, on the other hand, had become an anachronism; she had locked herself away in a time warp, not moving on with the times, not dealing with the past, stuck in a blank sort of limbo where her true feelings were papered over most of the time—until Antonio Marcolini had reappeared in her life and turned her world upside down and inside out.

From that first moment when she had heard his voice speak her name on the phone everything had changed. The feelings she had tried to squash had risen to the surface. They were bubbling even now, like volcanic mud, great big blobs of feeling, spluttering, popping with blistering heat, unpredictable, driven by forces outside of her control.

He kissed her mouth lingeringly, deeply and passionately, leaving her in a state of mindless, boneless need. Desire rippled through her as his tongue brushed against hers, calling hers into a sensual duel that left her gasping for more and more of his touch.

He moved his way down to each of her breasts, shaping them, moulding them with the warm broad palms of his hands, before taking each puckered nipple into his mouth. He rolled his tongue over the aching points in a circular motion, before sucking on them, his hot, wet mouth a delicious torture of feeling, sending shooting sparks of reaction to the very core of her being.

'You have such beautiful breasts,' he murmured as he trailed his mouth down to her belly button, circling it with the tip of his tongue. 'Everything about you is beautiful.'

Claire melted under the heat of his words. She had always considered herself an average-looking girl—not ugly, not supermodel material, but somewhere in between. Antonio made her feel as if she was the most gorgeous woman he had ever laid eyes on.

When he separated her tender folds with his fingers she flinched in response. 'Relax, *cara*,' he said softly. 'We have done this many times in the past, *si*?'

She still squirmed a little, her muscles tensing in spite of how gentle he was. 'I'm sorry,' she said on a scratchy breath. 'I'm not sure I can…'

'Do not be sorry, *tesoro mio*,' he said, stroking her inner thighs. 'We can take our time.'

Claire felt her heart swell. He was being so patient with her, just as he had been when they had first met. She had been reticent then, shy and uncertain of how to receive pleasure in such an intimate way, but he had patiently tutored every sensory nerve in her body, bringing every secret part of her to earth-shattering life.

After a moment she began to relax under the gentle caress of his hands. The movements against her smooth skin were slow but sure. It became increasingly obvious to her that he recalled all her pleasure spots. He knew just where to touch, how hard, how soft, how fast and how slow. She felt her body respond with small flutters beneath her skin to begin with, and then, as he stroked against her moist cleft, a wave began to build, higher and higher, gathering momentum, until that final moment when he brushed against the swollen pearl of her arousal again and again, in a soft flickering motion, triggering an orgasm so intense she gasped out in shocked surprise and wonder, her hands clutching at him as she rode out the storm of tumultuous feeling.

When she had calmed, Antonio tucked a springy chestnut curl of her hair behind the shell of her ear, his fingers lingering over the curve of her cheek. She looked so beautiful lying there, her dark lashes like tiny fans over her eyes, her breathing still hectic, her mouth still swollen and blood-red from his kisses.

Would he ever get enough of her to be able to let her go for good? he wondered. Was that why he hadn't pressed for a divorce? Was that why he had let things slide, putting his life on hold in a subconscious hope she would one day return to him? He had used her brother as a tool to get her back in his bed, but now he felt as if he had short-changed himself in some way. She was only with him now because she'd believed she had no choice. Once she realised how much she stood to gain if they were to divorce, would she use it against him in an act of revenge?

He drew her closer into his embrace, his body aching to have her again, but she was drifting off to sleep and he would have to wait. Then he felt her hand reach for him, her soft sigh of satisfaction at finding him hard and pulsing making him snatch in a breath of anticipation. He closed his eyes as she worked her magic on him, every sensitive nerve responding to her touch. He let her carry on for as long as he dared before he pulled her hand away and flipped her on to her back, driving into her warmth so deeply she clutched at him to steady his pace.

'I am sorry,' he said, instantly stilling his movements. 'Have I hurt you?'

'No,' she said, kissing his mouth in little feather-like kisses. 'You just took me by surprise, that's all.'

Antonio smiled against the press of her mouth. 'You took me by surprise too, *cara*,' he said, slowly building his rhythm until she was quivering in his arms.

He closed his eyes and felt himself lift off, the convulsions of her body triggering his own release, making him realise again how much he had missed her and how he would do anything to keep her right where he had her.

In his arms, in his bed, for as long as he could.

CHAPTER TEN

CLAIRE could feel the pain ripping through her, the stomping march of each contraction tearing apart her abdomen. She clutched at her stomach, her eyes springing open when she realised it was flat, not distended.

Sweat was pouring off her—tiny, fast-running rivulets coursing down between her heaving breasts—and the darkness of the strange bedroom only added to her sense of disorientation and deep-seated panic.

'Claire?' Antonio's deep voice came out of the thick cloak of darkness, and she felt the mattress beside her shift as he reached for the bedside lamp.

The muted glow was of some comfort, but Claire could still feel her heart thumping so heavily she was sure it would burst out of her ribcage. She held her hands against her breasts, just to make sure, her breathing coming in choking gasps.

'I...I had a bad dream...' she said through still trembling lips. 'A nightmare...'

Antonio frowned and, hauling himself into a sitting position, reached for her, gathering her close. 'Do you want to talk about it?' he asked against the fragrant silk of her hair.

She shook her head against his chest.

He began stroking the back of her head, her unruly curls tickling his palm. 'Dreams are not real, *cara*,' he said. 'It is just the brain processing a thousand images or more into some sense of order. Some of it makes sense; a lot of it does not. Dreams are not prophetic; they are just the workings of our deep unconscious at rest.'

She pulled back from him and looked into his eyes, hers wide with anguish. 'It's not the first time it's happened,' she said. 'I feel like she's crying out to me. I *hear* her, Antonio. I sometimes hear her crying for me, but I can't get to her.'

Antonio felt his throat thicken. Five years on and he knew exactly what Claire meant. He could fill his days and even his nights with totally mind-consuming work, and yet in those eerie, unguarded moments, late at night or in the early hours of the morning, he could hear her too. A soft mewing cry that ripped at his guts and left them raw and bleeding.

'I'm sorry...' Claire's soft voice penetrated the silence. 'I'm keeping you awake, and you probably have another big theatre list tomorrow.'

He continued stroking her hair. 'Try and go back to sleep, *cara*,' he said. 'I am used to sleepless nights. It is part of my job.'

After a while Antonio heard the deep and even sound of her breathing, but he didn't move her out of his arms. She had her head nestled against his chest, and his left arm was almost completely numb from the press of her slim body, but he didn't dislodge it or her. He lay staring blankly at the ceiling, his fingers still playing with her hair, his heart feeling as if a heavy weight was pressed down upon it.

It wouldn't take her long to realise he had never had any intention of pressing charges against Isaac. Once Claire knew she no longer had a compelling reason to stay with him as his wife, he would have to think of some other way of keeping her chained to his side. Not because of his father's will, not even because of the money she had taken from his mother, but because he wanted to wake up each morning just like this, with her warm and soft against him.

When Claire woke to find she was alone in Antonio's bed she felt a wave of disappointment wash over her. She wasn't sure what she had been expecting. Breakfast in bed with an avowal of love and red roses on the side was the stuff of dreams; it had no relevance to their current set-up.

She flung the covers back and got up, wincing as her inner muscles protested at the movement. It gave her a fluttery, excited sort of feeling inside to remember how passionately they had made love.

Had sex, she corrected herself. This was not about love—at least not from Antonio's point of view. This was about a physical attraction that had suddenly resurfaced.

Claire turned on the shower, a frown pulling at her forehead as she waited for the temperature to adjust.

Yes, but *why* had his attraction for her suddenly resurfaced? He had not sought her out until she had tried to serve those divorce papers on him. And by returning to live with him she had postponed any prospect of a divorce being processed smoothly. This reconciliation was not about working through the issues of the past; this was about a very rich man who did not want his inheritance cut straight down the middle. He could very well string her along indefinitely; she had already demonstrated to him how easily she could be won over. She cringed at how she had responded so freely to him the night before. She hadn't lasted twenty-four hours in his company without caving in to her need of him. How he must have gloated over her ready capitulation. She might even now be pregnant. She would have that whole heartache to go through again—tied to him for the sake of a child, never knowing if he wanted her for her, or for what she could give him.

When she had showered and dressed she found the note he had written next to the tea-making facilities in the suite, informing her he had an early list at one of the large teaching hospitals and would see her for a late dinner at around eight to eight-thirty that evening. There were no words of affection, no *I love you and can't wait to see you* phrases—nothing for her to hang her hopes on. She crumpled the note and tossed it in the bin, annoyed with herself for wishing and hoping for what she couldn't have.

Downstairs in the car park a few minutes later, Claire hoisted her handbag over her shoulder and narrowed her gaze at the parking attendant. 'What do you mean, this is *my* car?' she asked.

The parking valet smiled and handed her a silver embossed keyring. 'It is, Mrs Marcolini,' he said. 'Your husband had it delivered late yesterday. If you would like me to go through all the features with you, I would be happy to explain them—'

Claire plucked the keys from his hand. 'That will not be necessary,' she said with a proud hitch of her chin. 'A car is a car. I am sure I will be able to work out where the throttle and the brakes are.'

'Yes, but—'

She gave the young man a quelling look over her shoulder as she got behind the wheel. She took a moment to orientate herself. The new-car smell was a little off-putting—not to mention the butter-soft leather of the seats. Then there was the dashboard, with all its lights and gadgets, which looked as if it had been modelled on the latest space shuttle from NASA. Maybe she had been a little hasty in sending the helpful assistant on his way, she thought ruefully. After her old and battered jalopy, this car looked as if it needed a rocket scientist to set it in gear, let alone start it.

She took a deep breath and inserted the key that didn't even look like a key into the ignition. The car started with a gentle purr of the engine, its side mirrors opening outwards as if by magic, and the seatbelt light flashing to remind her to belt up.

'All right, already,' Claire muttered, and strapped herself in with a click.

OK, so where was the handbrake? It wasn't in between the driver and passenger seats, so where the hell was it?

The parking valet tapped on the window. Claire pursed her lips and hunted for the mechanism to lower the window, locking all the doors and popping the boot open before she finally located the button with the little window symbol on it.

'There's a foot brake on the left,' the man said with

a deadpan expression. 'And the release is that button on the right, marked brake release.'

Claire mentally rolled her eyes. 'Thank you,' she said, stiff with embarrassment. 'Have a nice day.'

The valet smiled and stepped well back. 'Have a nice drive.'

'Oh, my God.' Rebecca's eyes ran over the showroom-perfect gunmetal-grey of the vehicle Claire had parked outside the salon. 'You're driving a sports car?'

Claire dumped her handbag on the counter and sent her hand through her disordered curls. 'Yes, well, you *could* call it driving, I suppose,' she said wryly. 'Not that I had to do too much. The slightest spot of drizzle has the windscreen wipers coming on without me having to leaf through the manual to locate the appropriate switch. Apparently there's some sort of sensor that detects moisture. Going through the city tunnel, the headlights came on automatically—and turned off again once I was back out in daylight. And just now, parking between that florist's van and that utility, all I had to do was listen to the beeps and watch the flashing red lights as the parking assist device told me when I was getting too close.'

Rebecca let out a whistling stream of air through her teeth. 'Gosh, I wish *my* estranged husband would buy me a sports car. All he has given me so far is a lawyer's bill for the division of assets, most of which *I* own, since I was the only one with a full-time job the whole time we were together.'

Claire hid her scowl as she shrugged herself out of her coat and hung it on a hook in the back room. Rebecca was right. She shouldn't really be complaining about such a generous gift. Most women would be falling over themselves to have been given such a luxurious vehicle. Besides, Antonio had openly expressed his concern over her driving a less than roadworthy car. She didn't fool herself his concerns were for her safety, it was his reputation he was most concerned about—he had said as much at the time. But wouldn't it be wonderful if he had done it out of love for her? Money was no object for him, it never had been, so how could he know what such a gift would mean to her if the right motives had been behind it?

'You have a full list of clients today,' Rebecca said, when Claire came out of the back room into the salon. 'It seems everyone wants to be styled by the woman who has stolen the heart of Antonio Marcolini, celebrity surgeon *extraordinaire*.'

Claire organised her cutting and styling trolley with meticulous care. 'He's just a normal man, Bex,' she said, keeping her gaze averted. 'He brushes his teeth and shaves every morning, just like most other men.'

'So what's it like being back with him?' Rebecca asked. 'I read in the paper you've moved into his hotel suite with him.'

Claire lined up her radial brushes with studious precision. 'That's because my flat is too small. He is used to living in the lap of luxury. A one-bedroom flat in a tawdry inner-city suburb is hardly his scene. Moving in with him seemed the best option—for the time being, at least.'

'Have you done the deed with him yet?'

Claire couldn't control the hot flush of colour in her cheeks. In fact she could feel her whole body heating up at the memory of what she had done to him and what he had done to her.

'Bex, don't ask me questions like that,' she said, frowning heavily. 'There are some things even best mates have to keep private.'

Rebecca perched on the nearest stool and crossed her booted ankles. 'So that's a yes,' she said musingly. 'I thought as much. As soon as he came in here I knew you were a goner. He's hardly the sort of man you could say no to, is he?'

Claire put on her most severe schoolmistress sort of frown. 'This is just a trial reconciliation between us,' she said. 'Nothing has been decided in the long term. Just because he bought me a car it doesn't mean he wants me back for ever. For all I know it could be a consolation prize for when he hotfoots it back to Italy without me.'

Rebecca's forehead creased. 'But I thought you were still in love with him,' she said. 'You are, aren't you? Don't shatter all my romantic delusions, Claire. I'm counting on you to get me back into the dating pool with hope not despair as my personal floating device.'

Claire decided to come clean. 'It's a farce, Bex,' she said on an expelled breath. 'I'm not really back with Antonio. Not in the real sense.'

Rebecca narrowed her gaze. 'But you've all but admitted you slept with him,' she said. 'If that isn't being back together, what is? And what about that kiss in here yesterday, huh? That looked pretty full-on and genuine to me.'

'He's only here for three months,' Claire said flatly. 'There's no way I would go back to Italy with him unless I was absolutely sure he cared something for me, and quite frankly I can't see that happening. He's not the "I love you" type. I had his baby, for God's sake, and he never once said how he felt about me. Doesn't that tell you something?'

Rebecca grimaced. 'I guess when you put it like that…'

Claire blew out a breath. 'His father is dead. He died just a couple of months ago. I have reason to believe that is why Antonio is here now—not just to do the lecture tour, but to see what gives where I am concerned.'

'So what does give?' Rebecca asked with a pointed look.

Claire looked away and started realigning her brushes again, even though they were all neatly spaced on the trolley. 'I'm not sure,' she said, fiddling with a teasing comb, running her fingers across its pointed teeth, the movement making a slight humming noise. 'A divorce has always been on the cards. For all this time I have been waiting for him to make the first move, but he didn't. I decided to take matters into my own hands once I heard he was coming here, but now I wish I had let sleeping dogs lie.'

'Have you ever asked yourself *why* he never asked you for a divorce?' Rebecca asked after a small pause.

Claire continued to turn the comb over in her hands. 'What happened back then was…' She stopped for a moment, thinking about why Antonio had not sought his freedom as soon as he could. If he *had* been involved with Daniela Garza, why wouldn't he have activated a divorce as soon as possible, so he could be with the woman he wanted to be with? Everything pointed to Claire having got it horribly wrong about him. It didn't sit well with her to be in the guilty seat—that was the position she had always assigned *him*.

'Or, more to the point, have you ever asked yourself why you didn't divorce him?' Rebecca added.

Claire let out her breath on a sigh. 'I think you have probably guessed why.'

Rebecca gave her a look. 'So you *do* still love him? I sort of guessed you did. It's the way you say his name and the look you get in your eyes.'

Claire dropped the comb back on the trolley. 'All this time I've been fooling myself I hate him, but I don't. I love him. I have always loved him. I was so convinced he'd been having an affair, but he's always denied it.'

'Yeah, well, men do that, you know.'

Claire chewed at her lip. 'I don't know… Antonio is a good man, Bex. He does a lot of charitable work all over the globe. The more I think about it the more I start to doubt myself. What if I made a terrible mistake? What if he wasn't having an affair? What if he's been telling the truth the whole time? What have I done?'

'Claire, lots of marriages survive an affair, or even the suspicion of one,' Rebecca said. 'If he had one it must be well and truly over now—otherwise he wouldn't be with you, trying to sort things out. Give him a chance. You love him. Isn't that all that matters?'

'I'm not sure if he will ever feel anything for me,' Claire said. 'You can't exactly force someone to fall in love with you. If it happens, it happens.'

Rebecca raised her brows and flicked her gaze to the shiny new car outside. 'Listen, honey, any man who buys a woman a car like that must feel something for her. Just go with the flow for a while. Stop agonising over what you haven't got and enjoy what you have got. Some men are just not able to put their feelings into words; it's their actions you have to listen to.'

Claire glanced back at the car outside and sighed. How she wished Rebecca was right—that Antonio was showing her, not telling her how he felt. But then she remembered how much was at stake for him if they were to divorce. Was the car part of the buttering-up process, to keep her sweet when it came to finally putting an end to their relationship?

'Oh, I almost forgot,' Rebecca said. 'Your mother called. She said she'd left a couple of messages on your mobile but you hadn't got back to her. I think she's a bit hurt you didn't call her about getting back with Antonio. Like everyone else, she read about it in the paper.'

Claire grimaced. 'I turned my phone to silent. I forgot to change it back. Oh, God, what am I going to say to her?'

'Tell her the truth,' Rebecca said. 'Tell her you love Antonio and are working at rebuilding your marriage. She's your mum, Claire. All she wants is for you to be happy.'

Claire wanted it too—so much that it hurt. But her happiness was dependent on securing Antonio's love, and unfortunately that was not in her hands.

Maybe Rebecca was right; she needed to learn to go with the flow, to enjoy what she had for as long as it was there to be had. Antonio might have had less than noble motives for bringing about their reconciliation, but perhaps this window of time was her chance to show him how much she loved him—in spite of how he felt about her...

CHAPTER ELEVEN

CLAIRE didn't go straight back to the hotel from work. She took a detour to the cemetery, stopping to buy a bunch of tiny pink roses first. She cleaned out the brass vase and refilled it with fresh water, arranging the roses with loving care before placing them on her little daughter's resting place. She felt the familiar tight ache in her chest as she looked at the inscription, hot tears blurring her vision so she could hardly read her baby's name.

'Sleep tight, darling,' she said softly as she finally prepared to leave.

The traffic was heavy on the way back, so by the time she got to the hotel it was much later than she had expected.

'Where the hell have you been?' Antonio barked at her as soon as she came in the door.

Claire let her bag slip to the floor. 'I...I was caught up in traffic.'

'For two hours?' he asked, his gaze hard as it collided with hers.

She ran her tongue over her lips. 'How do you know how long it's been?'

'I called in at the salon but you had already left,' he

said. 'I made the trip back here and it only took me fifteen minutes—and that was during peak hour.'

Claire slipped off her coat, trying her best not to be intimidated by his brooding demeanour. 'Thank you for the car,' she said. 'It's lovely. I took it for a bit of a drive.'

'Where to?' The question was accusatory, hostile almost.

'To the cemetery,' she said, holding his dark angry gaze. 'To visit our daughter.'

Claire saw his throat move up and down over a tight swallow, one of his hands scoring a rough pathway through the thickness of his hair as his gaze shifted away from hers.

'Forgive me,' he said in a gruff tone. 'I should not have shouted at you like that.'

'I would have told you where I was going, but I thought you were going to be late,' she said. 'You said so in the note you left for me this morning.'

His eyes came back to hers. 'We got through the list faster than I expected. One of the patients had to be put off until next week due to a clotting problem.'

The silence stretched for a lengthy moment.

Claire broke it by saying, 'I need to have a shower. I feel as if I am covered in hair clippings and dye.' She began to move past him, but he captured her arm on the way past, stopping her in her tracks.

'Claire.'

She looked up at him, the weariness she could see in his face making her heart melt. 'Yes?' she said, barely above a whisper.

'I have something for you,' he said, reaching into his trouser pocket with his other hand.

Claire held her breath as he handed her two velvet ring boxes. She opened the first one to find an exquisite diamond solitaire engagement ring glittering there. The second box contained an equally beautiful diamond-encrusted wedding ring. She knew even before she slipped them onto her finger that they would both be a perfect fit.

She looked up at him again once the rings were in place, but his expression was difficult to read. 'Thank you, Antonio,' she said softly. 'They're truly beautiful. They must have cost you a fortune.'

He gave an off-hand shrug of one of his broad shoulders. 'They are just props,' he said. 'I do not want people to think I am not able or willing to provide you with nice jewellery.'

Claire couldn't help feeling crushed, but tried not to show it on her face. 'I am sure no one would think you a neglectful husband after all the money you have spent on me in the last twenty-four hours.'

His eyes studied her for a pulsing moment. 'Why didn't you tell me you made a large cash donation to the neonatal unit at St Patrick's hospital a few weeks after you returned to Australia?' he asked.

Claire rolled her lips together, wondering how he had found out. She had asked the CEO at the time to keep her name off the records. He had assured her no one would ever know who had made the donation.

'Claire?'

'How did you find out?' she asked.

'There are some secrets that are not so easy to keep,' he said, still with that inscrutable expression on his face.

Claire shifted under his steady gaze, absently twirling

the rings on her finger. 'You seem to have made it your business to find out everything you can about me.' She looked up at him again and asked, 'Should I be checking over my shoulder for a man in a trenchcoat?'

The line of his mouth grew tense. 'I would like you to inform me of your movements in future.'

Claire felt her back come up. 'Why?' she asked. 'So you can monitor my every move like a prisoner being kept under guard?'

'I would just like to know where you are and who you are with,' he said. He paused for a moment before adding, 'I was worried about you this evening.'

'Worried?' she asked with a lift of her brows. 'About my welfare or about whether I had escaped your clutches?'

His jaw visibly tightened as he held her gaze with the coal-black hardness of his. 'If you are harbouring the thought of leaving just remember it will only take one phone call to put your brother behind bars.'

Claire's gaze flicked to his mobile phone. 'You won't be able to hold that particular gun to my head for ever you know,' she said. 'It's already wearing a little thin, don't you think?'

He stepped towards her, tilting up her face, his eyes locking once again with hers. 'As long as it works for now,' he said, and slowly and inexorably lowered his mouth to hers.

Claire shivered as he deepened the kiss, her arms snaking around his neck, her senses firing on all cylinders. His tongue teased hers into a sexy tango, building her desire for him with each sensual movement. She pressed herself closer, her body singing with delight as she felt his arousal growing hot and hard against her. His hands skimmed down her sides, grasping her by the hips and pulling her even closer.

His kiss became more drugging, the sweep and caress of his tongue making her sigh with mounting pleasure. His hands moved from her waist to the undersides of her breasts, his thumbs close enough to rub across her nipples in tantalising back and forth movements that brought another whimper of delight from her in spite of the barrier of her clothes.

'I want you naked,' he said against her mouth. 'Now.'

Claire quivered as his hands cupped her breasts. 'I really need a shower…'

'Good idea,' he said, and lifted her effortlessly in her arms, carrying her through to the bathroom. 'I need one too.'

Claire wasn't sure who undressed who, but it seemed only seconds before they were standing under the hot spray of the shower, his mouth doing knee-trembling things to the sensitive skin at the side of her neck. She tilted her head and closed her eyes in bliss as his lips and tongue began an excruciatingly slow journey towards the swell of her breasts.

She was gasping by the time he got there, her senses screaming in reaction as his teeth gently scraped her sensitised flesh. He took her in his mouth, drawing on her, sucking and licking until every nerve was alive and jumping with feeling. The rasp of his stubbly jaw against her tender skin as he moved to her other breast made her spine tingle and her legs threaten to fold beneath her.

The steady stream of steamy water intensified the sensual feelings of their bodies rubbing against each other. Claire had showered with Antonio in the past, but she could not remember it feeling as exhilarating as this. Even as her excitement was building he was taking his time, as if he wanted to draw out every second of pleasure, and her body was delighting in it. Her anticipation grew and grew, making her breath come in breathless little pants as he came closer and closer to possessing her.

'Now…oh, please now,' she said, pressing herself against his hot, hard heat.

He held her slightly aloft, teasing her with his length at her moist entrance. Just waiting for that first plunge into her tight warmth made her heart race in feverish expectation.

'Tell me how much you want me,' he said, rubbing himself against her.

The erotic motion drove every thought but his imminent possession out of her head. 'Don't make me beg, Antonio,' she gasped as he brushed against her again. 'You know how much I want you. I have never wanted anyone but you.'

His eyes gleamed with male satisfaction as he pressed her back against the shower stall, positioning her for his entry.

Claire closed her eyes as he surged forward, her body accepting him with slick wet heat, her tight muscles clamping around him, drawing him in. He started slowly, but his pace increased until she was breathing as heavily as him, her hands grasping at him to keep her upright as her body began to splinter into a thousand pieces, each one trembling, spinning and quivering in a maelstrom of sensation.

He came within seconds of her, his low, deep grunts of pleasure making her skin pepper all over with goose-bumps as he spilled himself. She felt his body shiver under the pads of her fingertips as she ran them lightly over his back, his taut muscles twitching in the aftermath.

Antonio finally stepped back and brushed the wet hair out of her face. 'I will let you finish up in here,' he said, running a gentle fingertip over a patch of redness on the upper curve of her breast. 'I need to have a shave before I take any more of your skin off.'

Claire looked at her breast, the startling contrast of its creamy softness against the dark tan of his finger making her stomach tilt all over again. She drew in a tight little breath as his fingertip brushed over her nipple, and then another as he circled her areola.

His eyes meshed with hers. 'Did you see your doctor about contraception?' he asked.

Claire felt as if he had just turned the cold water on. She stared at him, her heart-rate not quite steady. 'No…I haven't been able to get an appointment.'

'Where are you in your cycle?'

'I'm not sure…'

His eyes were still locked on hers. 'We have had un-protected sex several times now. Has it occurred to you that you could have already conceived a child?'

She swallowed thickly and, reaching past him, turned off the shower. She stepped out of the cubicle and snatching up one of the big fluffy towels, wrapped herself in it. 'I thought you said the other day it was not the right time to be talking about babies?' she said.

He wrapped a towel around his hips. 'That was then. This is now.'

She eyed him suspiciously. 'So what's changed?' she asked.

'We are older and wiser, Claire. Things could work for us.'

Claire searched his face for some clue to what he was feeling, but his expression was mask-like. 'So…' She paused as she moistened her mouth. 'So what you are saying is…you want to stay married?'

'It was never my intention to divorce you, Claire.'

'Why?' she asked. 'Because it could prove too costly for you now your father has died and left you half of everything he owned?'

Something flickered in his eyes. 'That is why you issued me with the divorce papers, was it not?' he asked. 'You saw a chance to take me to the cleaners in return for all the ways I had supposedly let you down in the past. Do not forget I saw the newspaper article too, Claire. It mentioned the recent death of my father. You did the sums, but fortunately for me your brother took matters into his own hands.'

Claire glared at him, her hands going to tight fists by her sides. 'You bastard. The first I heard about your father's death was when you told me at our first meeting,' she said through clenched teeth. 'You arrogant, unfeeling bastard. Right from the start you set out to seduce me back into your bed, hoping once I was there again I wouldn't want to leave. No wonder you've been buying me expensive rings and a car and talking about babies. You wanted to make me think twice about leaving.'

'There is not going to be a divorce, Claire,' he said, with an intransigent set to his mouth. 'I want you to be absolutely clear about that—especially if there is going to be a child.'

'How can you be so clinical about this?' she asked. 'This is not some business deal. This is my life you're talking about. What if I want to spend it with someone else? Have you thought about that?'

His eyes pinned hers. 'Is there someone else?'

She sent him a resentful scowl. 'Why don't you tell me? You're the one keeping tabs on me.'

'I am not keeping tabs on you,' he said heavily. 'I found out quite by accident you were responsible for that donation. It threw me to think you had not thought to tell me. You allowed me to think you had taken money from my mother to indulge yourself; instead I find that you have been responsible for saving perhaps hundreds of premature babies' lives.'

'I didn't ask your mother for the money. She had written the cheque before she came to see me that night. I am not sure why she continues to insist I demanded it from her.'

Antonio released a sigh. 'There is no point in going over this again. If you say that is how it happened, then I am prepared to leave it at that.'

Her blue-green eyes widened in surprise. 'You believe me?'

'If we are to make a success of our marriage this time around we will both have to learn to trust each other,' he said, dragging a hand through his still-damp hair.

She gave him an ironic look. 'You just accused me of trying to take half your assets. Doesn't that imply a lack of trust on your part?'

He looked at her for a long moment. 'Why, after all

this time, did you wait until now to ask me for a divorce?' he asked.

She captured her lip, chewed at it for a second or two before she answered. 'I believed our marriage to be well and truly over, that's why.'

Even now Antonio wondered if he could believe her. He had blackmailed her back into his bed, but she was right in saying he couldn't hold the threat of her brother's imprisonment over her indefinitely. He should not have held it over her in the first place. Her brother had acted out of a sense of loyalty—the kind of behaviour he had seen in his own brother Mario time and time again.

Antonio's head was still reeling with the shock of finding out Claire had not used that money for her own gain. Five years of brooding anger had been swept away with a single sentence from a virtual stranger who had known more about his wife than he did.

It was like seeing Claire for the first time; he was discovering things about her he had not noticed before. Like how she kissed with her whole body, not just her mouth. And how gentle her hands were, the way they sent electrical charges through him with the simplest touch. How sweet her rare smile was, how it touched him in a way nothing else had done. How her beautiful eyes glittered with anger and defiance one moment, then brimmed with emotion at the mere mention of their baby daughter the next. She was like a movie or a novel he had not understood the first time around. She had layers and sub-plots that made him appreciate her uniqueness in a way he had never done before.

He had never been comfortable identifying his

emotions concerning Claire. He still wasn't sure why. It wasn't as if he'd had a difficult background, or had suffered at the hands of another woman, therefore making it difficult to let his guard down. He just knew he felt something for Claire he had not felt for any other woman.

He tipped up her chin and brushed his mouth with hers. 'It is not over, *cara*,' he said, and unhooked her towel, tossing it to the floor along with his. 'Not by a long shot.'

CHAPTER TWELVE

THREE weeks later Claire came out of the salon's bathroom to find Rebecca looking at her speculatively. 'Are you going to continue to fob me off by telling me it was something you ate, or are you going to come clean?' she asked. 'That is the third time in as many days you've been sick.'

Claire blew out a sigh as she dabbed at her clammy brow. 'I think I'm pregnant. I haven't had a test yet, but the signs are all there.'

Rebecca's eyes opened wide with excitement. 'Wow, Claire—that's fabulous! Have you told Antonio?'

Claire began to chew at her lip. 'No…not yet.'

'You don't think he'll be pleased?'

Claire met her friend's questioning gaze. 'I think he'll be very pleased,' she said. 'It means a divorce will be out of the question—for the time being at least.'

Rebecca frowned. 'But, hon, I thought a divorce was out of the question now anyway. The last couple of weeks you've been happier than I've seen you in years. I thought it was finally working out between you and Antonio.'

'It's true things have been much better between us,'

Claire said, thinking of how attentive and considerate Antonio had been lately. 'He's been lovely towards me—taking me out to dinners and shows, and buying me clothes and stuff. He even offered to drive to Narrabri next weekend to meet my mother.'

'But?'

Claire gave Rebecca an anguished look. 'Don't you see, Bex? It's happening all over again.'

'I'm not sure I'm following you…'

'The one thing Antonio wants is an heir,' Claire said. 'When I fell pregnant before that's why he insisted on marrying me—to give the baby his name. It wasn't about loving me or wanting to spend the rest of his life with me. It was about securing an heir for the Marcolini empire.'

'But, Claire, things might have changed now.'

'Oh, yes,' Claire said with a cynical twist of her mouth. 'They very definitely *have* changed. He is now in possession of half his father's wealth as well as his own, which is no small fortune, let me tell you. He knows if he divorces me he will have to give me a huge cut of it. What better way to keep his money than to lure me back into his life and get an heir in the process?'

Rebecca shifted her pursed lips from side to side for a moment. 'I'm thinking you haven't told him you still love him. Am I right?'

'Oh, Bex, I have to bite my tongue every single day,' Claire choked, close to tears. 'But that's the mistake I made before. I can't make myself so vulnerable again. If we are to stay together I want it to be on equal terms. I want to be loved not for what I can give him, but for me—just me.'

'Claire, it's only been…what…a little over three

weeks or so since you got back together?' Rebecca said. 'And don't forget his feet had barely stepped on Australian soil when you started waving divorce papers under his nose. He's not likely to unveil his feelings in a hurry after something like that.'

'I guess you're right…' Claire said as she sat on the stool at the reception counter and put her head in her hands. 'It hasn't exactly been a textbook reunion.'

Rebecca stood behind her and gave her shoulders a little squeeze. 'Why don't you take a couple of weeks off? You should get some rest in any case. Then, when you're all relaxed and not feeling so unsure of yourself, you can tell Antonio about the baby.'

Claire got off the stool and faced her friend. 'I think I will take a few days off,' she said. 'I don't want anything to go wrong with this pregnancy. I just couldn't bear it.'

Antonio had not long finished his last case when he received a phone call from his brother Mario, back in Rome. He rubbed his hand across the stubble on his jaw as he listened to the news he had been dreading ever since he'd boarded the plane to Australia.

'How long do the doctors think she will last?' he asked as he stripped off his theatre cap and tossed it in the bin.

'It is hard to say—a week, maybe less,' Mario responded. 'She has been asking for you.'

Antonio felt his insides clench. The irony was particularly painful. The last time he had seen his mother she had looked at him blankly, asking the home care nurse who this tall, dark and handsome stranger was. 'I will arrange a flight straight away,' he informed his brother.

'Is your runaway wife coming with you?' Mario asked.

Antonio felt his teeth grind together at his brother's sardonic tone. 'Claire will take some convincing, but, yes, I plan to bring her with me,' he answered. 'And I would appreciate it if you would not mention the past again. We are getting along just fine.'

'So you have so far managed to stop her divorcing you?' Mario asked.

'So far,' Antonio said, thinking of all the times in the last couple of weeks when he had caught Claire looking at him in that covert way of hers, her gaze immediately falling away from his as if she was harbouring a guilty secret.

For all his talk that day of developing trust between them, he could not get past the thought that she might very well be planning the best payback of all. He couldn't quite shake the feeling, no matter how he tried. Even though she shared his bed willingly, with as much if not more enthusiasm as before, she never once mentioned her feelings towards him as she'd used to do so freely in the past. Even her smiles were fleeting and distant, as if her mind was occupied elsewhere. The only place he could get and hold her full attention was in bed. It was there she responded to him without holding back, her body convulsing around his as he claimed her again and again. He had thought his attraction to her would burn itself out, but it had done the very opposite. He wanted her more than he had ever wanted her. His physical need of her was so great at times it was overwhelming. The irony was that it had been all he had wanted from her in the beginning, and yet now, when he was so sure he could have it, he wanted so much more.

When Antonio got back to the hotel Claire was sitting

in the lounge with her legs curled beneath her, a magazine in her lap.

'Hi,' she said, closing the pages as he came in.

'Hi, yourself,' he said, bending down to kiss her briefly.

She looked at him warily once he had straightened. 'Is something wrong?' she asked, unfolding her legs and placing her feet on the carpeted floor, her hands gripping the sofa until her knuckles showed through her creamy skin.

'Claire, I have to return to Italy,' he said without preamble. 'I need to go as soon as possible. I want you to come with me.'

'No,' she said, instantly springing to her feet.

He frowned as she suddenly paled before him, her body swaying slightly. He put out a hand and steadied her. '*Cara*, I did not mean to spring that on you like that, but—'

'I don't want to go.' She cut him off, her face still deathly pale.

'What is wrong?' he asked, still holding her.

'I told you from the start I am not moving back to Italy with you,' she said with a stubborn set to her mouth. 'You can't make me go.'

'I thought we had an agreement,' he said, holding her defiant gaze.

She glared at him, but he could see a nerve flickering at the side of her mouth.

'Don't try and blackmail me, Antonio. It's not going to work. I was speaking to Isaac only yesterday. Your friend has helped him apply for a youth worker's course. He starts in a couple of weeks. He told me you were the one who paid his fees. There is no way you would turn him in now—not unless you don't have an ounce of compassion in your soul.'

Antonio silently ground his teeth as he tried to think of another way to convince her. In the end he decided to try another tactic—to reveal a side of him she had never seen before. 'Claire, my mother is dying,' he said heavily. 'I need to go to her. She is asking for me.'

She shifted under his gaze, her tongue darting out to moisten her lips. 'Go on your own. You don't need me there.'

'I would like you to be there, *tesoro mio*,' he said, scraping a hand through his hair. *I need you to be there.*

'I am quite sure your mother would prefer it if I didn't intrude on such a painfully private moment,' she said, but her voice had lost its hardened edge. Her eyes, too, had softened, bringing out the rich blueness of them.

'The point is my mother will probably not even recognise you.'

She frowned at him. 'What do you mean?'

He released a weary sigh. 'My mother is suffering from Alzheimer's. Up until recently she has been cared for at home by a nurse, but early this morning, Italian time, she suffered a stroke. Her memory of the past, which was already rapidly declining, is now virtually non-existent.'

'But I thought you said she specifically asked for you?' she said.

'She did—which is why it is imperative I go to her,' he said. 'Patients with Alzheimer's can still have short periods of lucidity. I want to see her. It is important to me. I was not there for my father. I did not get to say the things I wanted to say. I did not get to hear the things he wanted to say to me.' He paused for a moment. 'I was not there for you and our baby either. That is something I will regret for the rest of my life. I do not want any more regrets, Claire. Please…do this one thing for me.'

Claire felt her rigid stance begin to crumble. She could see this was a very difficult time for him. He had not long ago lost his father, and now his mother was desperately ill. It was impossible for her to deny him this one request. And hearing him speak of their little baby with such emotion in his voice went a long way to healing the hurt she had carried for so long. Although he had said nothing to her about it, she knew he had gone to visit their daughter's resting place. When she had gone there today, after she had left the salon, she had found a teddy bear dressed in a pink tutu propped up next to a huge bunch of flowers, and a card written in both English and Italian: *With all my love, your devoted Papà.*

It had made Claire realise how private a person Antonio was. He had lived most of his life under the intrusive glare of the paparazzi, and when he grieved he liked to do so alone. If only she had recognised that all those years ago. He was not one to express his feelings to all and sundry. He kept things inside, working through them at his own pace, locking a part of himself away to cope with the difficult issues he had to deal with on a daily basis. How could he handle the welfare of his patients if he was to fall apart emotionally all the time? Patients did not need a surgeon to cry with them. They needed a competent, caring specialist who could think clearly and make good clinical decisions about their condition and how best to deal with it.

It was a shock to realise how little she had known

Antonio in the past—how little she had understood of him as a man and as a gifted surgeon. She had fallen in love with a small part of him, never realising the true depths of his character until now.

'Claire, I do not expect to be away for more than a week or ten days at the most,' Antonio assured her. 'I still have commitments here, although they have had to be rescheduled for when I return.'

'All right,' she said on a little sigh. 'I will come with you.'

He pressed a soft kiss to the middle of her forehead. 'Thank you, *il mio amato*,' he said. 'I will try and make things as comfortable for you as possible.'

The flight to Rome was long, but Claire slept on and off in the executive suite Antonio had arranged on the plane. She woke once during the flight to find him lying fully clothed on top of the covers beside her, staring at the ceiling, his handsome features so drawn with exhaustion her heart went out to him.

She stroked a gentle hand across his stubbly jaw. 'Why don't you get undressed and lie down for a while?'

He turned his head and gave her a rueful smile. 'If I get into that bed with you, sleep will be the last thing on my mind.'

Claire felt her cheeks start to glow. 'Maybe that's exactly what you need right now,' she said softly. 'Maybe it's what we both need.'

He rolled on his side and brushed her hair back from her forehead, his eyes dark and intense as they meshed with hers. She closed her eyes as his mouth came down, the brush of his tongue against hers setting her instantly alight. With her mouth still locked on his, she worked the buttons of his shirt, pulling it off him with impatient fingers. She attacked his belt and trousers with the same passionate intent, aching to feel his body against hers without the barrier of clothes.

Antonio removed the slip of a nightgown she was wearing, kissing her breasts, rolling his tongue over each ripe berry of her nipples, his teeth tugging and his tongue soothing simultaneously, his mouth a hot brand of possession that drove her wild with need.

His erection was thick and throbbing against her moist entrance, his breathing ragged as he fought for control. 'I should put on a condom,' he said, reaching across to rummage in his bag. 'You will not be totally covered by the pill yet. It has only been a couple of weeks, *si*?'

Claire stroked his arm with her fingers, her eyes falling away from his. She had let him think she had gone ahead with the appointment with her doctor, and now she wished she hadn't lied by omission. But telling him about her pregnancy now didn't seem quite like the right time. She wanted to feel more assured of his feelings for her. Anyway, it was very early days; anything could go wrong at this stage. She hadn't even had it confirmed in case she jinxed something. She wanted to wait until she was absolutely sure she wasn't imagining it before she told him.

'I am sure it will be fine,' she said. 'I want to feel you.'

He positioned himself over her and she welcomed him with a gasp of delight, moving with him, catching his rhythm, her body gripping him greedily. He reached between their rocking bodies to stroke the moist centre of her desire, his fingers finding their target with consummate ease. She was so ready for him, her back arching off the mattress to keep him where she wanted him. He drew out the pleasure for her, changing his touch to tease her into a cataclysmic release. She was approaching the summit. He could feel her inner muscles start to contract, her whimpering cries coming faster and faster as she finally let go. It was impossible for him to hold back. He surged forward with several deep, hard thrusts, spilling himself, shuddering with the sensation of ultimate pleasure as it flowed through him in waves.

The deep and even sound of Antonio's breathing had a soporific affect on Claire. Her eyes felt as if they were weighted by anvils, and after a few attempts to keep them open she gave up with a soft sigh, and fell into a dreamless sleep curled up in his arms.

When Claire woke the pilot announced they were due to land.

The journey through Customs was tiresome, due to a security scare that had happened with a tourist a few days ago. Everyone seemed to be on tenterhooks, which was quite understandable, and the checkpoints took much longer than normal, even for those holding an Italian passport.

Although the building was air-conditioned Claire felt clammy and, using a tissue, wiped beads of moisture from her forehead. Antonio glanced at her as they were being ushered through, his gaze narrowing in concern.

'Are you all right, *cara*?' he asked. 'The crowds are annoying, I know, but we will soon be home.'

Home.

He said it so naturally—as if it really was her home as well. But it would never be home for her—not unless she felt loved and accepted by him. She could live anywhere with him if he loved her the way she loved him. His heart was her home and always would be.

The trip to the Marcolini *palazzo* was lengthened by a traffic snarl, but soon enough the familiar sight came into view. The three-storey mansion stood in stately pride, and the lush green of trees and shrubbery, holding a host of hot summer fragrances, reminded Claire of the blisteringly dry and dusty Outback, where her mother vainly tried year after year to coax flowers and vegetables to grow.

The other startling difference from her background was the number of household staff the Marcolinis employed. Housekeepers—both junior and senior—a gardener and a pool maintenance man, not to mention a chauffeur who seemed to be on call twenty-four hours a day.

'Isn't your mother being looked after in hospital now?' Claire asked, automatically lowering her voice to the hushed, whispered tone all the staff she had encountered so far seemed to have adopted.

'No,' Antonio said. 'She expressly wished to be allowed to stay at home with her family around her.'

Claire looked up at the grand marble staircase to see Antonio's brother descending. Taller by an inch or two, he had the same dark good-looks of his older sibling, his body long and lean and toned by the gym and the pool. He had the same dark brown almost black eyes, but while Antonio's were often filled with compassion for the patients under his care, Mario's were hardened with the worldly cynicism he wore like a second skin.

'So the prodigal wife returns,' he said, as he came to

the foot of the stairs where Claire was standing. 'Welcome home, Claire.'

Antonio swore at his brother in Italian, changing back to English to ask, 'How is Mamma?'

'Conscious, but not making much sense,' Mario answered. 'She keeps thinking I am Papà.'

'Yes, well, you look more like him than me,' Antonio said, massaging the back of his neck, where he could feel a knot of tension the size of a golfball. 'Has anyone else been to visit?'

'Daniela came by yesterday, with her husband and baby son,' Mario informed him. 'I am not sure if she will be back,' he added, glancing briefly at Claire.

Claire felt her colour rise and bit down on her lip. Was she for ever to be reminded of her stupid mistake in believing her husband had betrayed her?

'I had better spend some time with Mamma,' Antonio said. 'Has her doctor been today?'

Mario nodded grimly. 'There is nothing you can do, Antonio. You are not her doctor; you are her son. You need to remember that.'

Antonio swallowed the lump of grief that had risen in his throat. 'Can you get Claire a drink and show her to our room? She is tired from the journey. She almost passed out coming through Customs.'

Claire felt her face flame with guilty colour all over again. She was sure Mario thought she had been putting it on, but she did still feel horribly faint and nauseous. A long-haul flight and crossing time zones, even if in the lap of luxury, was not conducive to feeling one hundred percent even without the suspicion of being pregnant. Even the sudden heat after the cool winter in

Sydney took some getting used to. Antonio himself looked ashen and tired beyond description, with dark shadows underscoring his eyes like bruises, but then he was facing the sadness of losing his mother so soon after the death of his father.

'What would you like to drink?' Mario asked as he led the way to the *salotto*.

'Do you have fresh orange juice?' Claire asked.

He gave her his playboy, teasing smile. 'Does Australia have bush flies?'

A reluctant smile tugged at Claire's mouth. She had to admit that Mario, when he let his guard down, could be utterly charming. It was no wonder Antonio would not hear a bad word said against him.

Mario handed her a glass of icy cold orange juice. 'So,' he said, running his gaze over her speculatively, 'you are reunited with my brother.'

Claire lowered her gaze. 'Yes…'

'Let's hope it lasts this time around,' he said. 'He has not been the same since you left.'

Claire took a deep breath and met his hardened gaze full-on. 'I love him, Mario. I know you probably don't believe it, but I do. I've been so stupid. I can't believe how stupid I was back then. I know he wasn't having an affair. I feel so sure of it now. I have never stopped loving him. Not for a moment. I love him so much.'

'Have you told him that?' Mario asked, stalling in the process of lifting his glass to his mouth.

'Have you told me what?' Antonio asked as he stepped into the room behind her.

Claire swung around to reply, but before she could

get the words into some sort of order she began to wobble on her feet, her vision blurring alarmingly. She tried to concentrate, to hold on to consciousness, but her extremities were already fizzing with the sudden loss of blood pressure. She felt herself falling, saw the marbled floor coming towards her with frightening speed. The glass she was holding slipped out of her grasp, shattering into a thousand pieces.

She vaguely registered Antonio's voice calling out, 'Catch her!' but if Mario did so in time she was totally unaware of it....

Claire woke in a darkened room. Her aching forehead was being stroked with a cool damp cloth by Antonio. 'What's going on?' she asked through dry lips. 'Where am I?'

'*Cara*, you hit your head when you fainted,' he said, concern thickening his voice. 'I want you to go to hospital to have it X-rayed. The ambulance is on its way. You could have fractured your skull.'

She felt her vision blurring again, and his words seemed to be coming from a long way off. Her head was pounding as if a construction site had taken up residence inside. She felt a wave of sickness rise in her throat, but managed to swallow it down just as the sound of a siren approached on the street outside.

As the ambulance officers loaded her into the back of the vehicle, Claire turned her head to look at Antonio, whose face was grey with anguish. 'I don't need you to come with me,' she said. 'You should be with your mother. How is she?'

'She is fine for now,' Antonio said, gently squeezing

her hand before tucking it back under the cotton blanket. 'She has even been asking for you.'

She blinked at him, even though it sent another jackhammer through her skull. 'She's been asking for *me*?' she asked in a shocked whisper. 'She…she knows I'm here…with you?'

'I told her we were together again,' he said. 'I think she wants to say goodbye and to apologise.'

Claire felt her heart contract even as her consciousness began to waver alarmingly again. 'Tell her…tell her to wait for me…'

'I will,' Antonio said, leaning forward to press a soft kiss to the paper-white skin of her brow just as her eyes fluttered downwards.

'*Come è lei?*'

Claire heard Antonio's voice ask how she was. But the answer from the doctor he was speaking with, even though delivered in the rather stilted manner of a non-Italian speaker, she found hard to follow in her disordered state, apart from the words for 'mild concussion.'

'Commozione minimo…um…er… Ma non è tutto… Lei è incinta…er…'

'How far along?' Antonio asked next—in English this time, clearly in an attempt to put his struggling colleague out of his misery.

Claire felt a prickly sensation go through her, as if all of her corpuscles had been injected with tiny bubbles of air, each one containing a particle of joy.

So it had been confirmed at last.

She was pregnant.

'Two weeks—maybe three,' the doctor answered

Antonio in English, his lilting accent giving him away as a Scot, obviously on a foreign medical rotation. 'She is obviously sensitive to the change in her hormones. Some women are more so than others, making the symptoms kick in much earlier than normal. The knock on the head will not help the morning sickness, of course, but with adequate rest she should pick up in a few days. I've had a quick look through her records. She will have to be closely monitored, given what happened last time, but it's entirely possible she will have a safe delivery of a healthy wee one this time. We have come a long way in the last five years in maternal health management.'

Claire felt her heart turn over inside her chest as the joy she was feeling began to spread right through her. If everything went right, she would in a matter of months be holding a baby in her arms—alive and breathing. Up until now she hadn't dared think too far ahead. It had been enough to suspect she was carrying Antonio's baby. To find out there was every reason to hope for a healthy delivery was nothing short of a miracle to her.

'*Grazie*,' Antonio said with a hitch in his voice. 'I mean—thank you.'

'No trouble. I am sorry to hear your mother is not well,' the doctor added. 'Perhaps news of a grandchild will be just the tonic she needs right now?'

'You could be right,' Antonio said. 'Thank you again. You have been very kind and attentive. It is greatly appreciated.'

Claire waited until the sound of the doctor's footsteps had faded into the distance before she opened her eyes. Antonio was looking down at her, his dark brown eyes meltingly soft.

'*Cara*.' His tone was gentle. 'The good news is you do not have a fracture of your skull.'

'And…and the bad news?'

He smiled. 'I do not consider it bad news at all. The doctor attending your admission has found you are pregnant. He took a set of routine blood tests and it came up positive. You're pregnant.'

Claire felt the tears rising until they were streaming down her face. She sniffed, and Antonio quickly reached over and plucked a tissue out of the box by her bed. He began to gently mop at her cheeks. 'And here I was, thinking you had gone on the pill,' he said in mock reproach.

'I was going to,' she said. 'I was about to call to make an appointment when I realised I was a couple of days late. I decided to wait and see.'

He began to frown. 'You *were* planning on telling me, were you not?'

'Of course!' she said. 'Surely you don't think…?'

He gave a rueful grimace. 'It would be no less than I deserved. I have not exactly been the best husband to you, have I?'

Claire lowered her gaze, plucking at the sheet with her fingers. 'I haven't exactly been the best wife…'

He picked up her hand and brushed his lips against her bent fingers. 'I cannot tell you how thrilled I am about the baby,' he said. 'It is the best news I could have hoped for.'

She gnawed at her lip for a moment. 'It's not just about keeping your inheritance?'

'It has never been about my inheritance,' he said, his eyes warm and soft as they held hers. 'I love you, *il mio amato uno*. I have been so stupid not to have recognised it for all this time. I was too proud to admit the woman I loved had left me. I should have fought for you, Claire. I realise that now. I should have moved heaven and earth to bring you back to me.'

Claire's heart swelled to twice its size as she fell forward into his arms. 'I love you too,' she sobbed against his broad, dependable chest. 'I've been such a fool. I can't believe I left you. It was so immature of me.'

'Hush, *cara*,' he soothed, stroking her back with a gossamer-light touch. 'You were still hurting. Losing Isabella was…' His voice caught but he went on. 'It was like being locked inside an abyss of grief so thick and dark it was all I could do to get through each day without breaking down completely. People were depending on me—my patients, my colleagues—and yet in all of it the most important person I should have supported was you. But I was too shell-shocked to face it at the time. Every time I looked at the pain in your eyes I felt my heart being ripped open. In the end I just could not bear to think what I had done to you. I got you pregnant. I did not support you the way you needed. And when Isabella did not make it I felt…I *still* feel…it was my fault.'

Claire lifted her eyes to his dark moist ones. 'You said her name…' Her voice came out on an incredulous whisper of sound. 'For the first time *ever* you said her name…twice…'

Antonio's throat moved up and down as he fought to control his emotions. 'I have wanted to so many times, *cara*,' he said. 'But every time I tried to I felt as if a giant hand had grasped me by the throat, squeezing until I could not breathe.'

Claire hugged him tightly, allowing him the chance to let out the grief that in her own ignorance and pain had not been allowed purchase.

It was a long time before either of them could speak, but when they finally came apart she looked into his red-rimmed eyes and felt a rush of sheer joy for the first time in five long, lonely years.

'My mother wishes to apologise in person for misleading you,' Antonio said. 'She really felt she was doing the right thing at the time. She thought you no longer loved me. That is why she gave you the money—to help you get back on your feet. She thought it might help you to cut loose by hinting Daniela and I were still involved. I hope you will find it in yourself to forgive her. I know it is a lot to ask. I am finding it hard to forgive her myself.'

Claire smiled as she stroked his raspy jaw. 'Of course I forgive her—and you must too. I do not want any bad feelings to get in the way of our happiness. Not after so long apart.'

He smiled and kissed her softly on her lips. 'I am the luckiest man on earth,' he said. 'I am over the moon about you being back in my life, about the baby, about being together again, about being a family.'

'Speaking of family,' she said. 'Isn't it time you got back to yours at the *palazzo*?'

'My family is right here,' he said, kissing her passionately. 'And I am not going to be separated from it again.'

* * * * *

Turn the page for an exclusive extract from
THE PRINCE'S CAPTIVE WIFE
by
Marion Lennox

Bedded and wedded—by blackmail!

Nine years ago Prince Andreas Karedes left
Australia to inherit his royal duties, but unbe-
knownst to him he left a woman pregnant.

Innocent young Holly tragically lost their baby
and remained on her parents' farm to be near her
tiny son's final resting place, wishing Andreas
would return!

A royal scandal is about to break: a dirt-digging
journalist has discovered Holly's secret, so
Andreas forces his childhood sweetheart to come
and face him! Passion runs high as Andreas issues
an ultimatum: to avoid scandal, Holly must
become his royal bride!

"SHE WAS ONLY SEVENTEEN?"

"We're talking ten years ago. I was barely out of my teens myself."

"Does that make a difference?" The uncrowned king of Aristo stared across his massive desk at his younger brother, his aquiline face dark with fury. "Have we not had enough scandal?"

"Not of my making." Prince Andreas Christos Karedes, third in line to the Crown of Aristo, stood his ground against his older brother with the disdain he always used in this family of testosterone-driven males. His father and brothers might be acknowledged womanizers, but Andreas made sure his affairs were discreet.

"Until now," Sebastian said. "Not counting your singularly spectacular divorce, which had a massive impact. But this is worse. You will have to sort it before it explodes over all of us."

"How the hell can I sort it?"

"Get rid of her."

"You're not saying…"

"Kill her?" Sebastian smiled up at his younger brother,

obviously rejecting the idea—though a tinge of regret in his voice said the option wasn't altogether unattractive.

And Andreas even sympathized. Since their father's death, all three brothers had been dragged through the mire of the media spotlight, and the political unrest was threatening to destroy them. In their thirties, impossibly handsome, wealthy beyond belief, indulged and feted, the brothers were now facing realities they had no idea what to do with.

"Though if I was our father…" Sebastian added, and Andreas shuddered. Who knew what the old king would have done if he'd discovered Holly's secret? Thank God he'd never found out. Not that King Aegeus could have taken the moral high ground. It was, after all, his father's past actions that had gotten them into this mess.

"You'll make a better king than our father ever was," Andreas said softly. "What filthy dealing made him dispose of the royal diamond?"

"That's my concern," Sebastian said. There could be no royal coronation until the diamond was found—they all knew that—but the way the media was baying for blood there might not be a coronation even then. Without the diamond the rules had changed. If any more scandals broke… "This girl…"

"Holly."

"You remember her?"

"Of course I remember her."

"Then she'll be easy to find. We'll buy her off—do whatever it takes, but she mustn't talk to anyone."

"If she wanted to make a scandal she could have done it years ago."

"So it's been simmering in the wings for years. To

have it surface now…" Sebastian rose and fixed Andreas with a look that was almost as deadly as the one used by the old king. "It can't happen, brother. We have to make sure she's not in a position to bring us down."

"I'll contact her."

"You'll go nowhere near her until we're sure of her reaction. Not even a phone call, brother. For all we know her phones are already tapped. I'll have her brought here."

"I can arrange…"

"You stay right out of it until she's on our soil. You're heading the corruption inquiry. With Alex on his honeymoon with Maria—of all the times for him to demand to marry, this must surely be the worst—I need you more than ever. If you leave now and this leaks, we can almost guarantee losing the crown."

"So how do you propose to persuade her to come?"

"Oh, I'll persuade her," Sebastian said grimly. "She's only a slip of a girl. She might be your past, but there's no way she's messing with our future."

* * * * *

Be sure to look for
THE PRINCE'S CAPTIVE WIFE
by Marion Lennox,
available September 2009
from Harlequin Presents®!

HARLEQUIN *Presents*

TWO CROWNS, TWO ISLANDS, ONE LEGACY

A royal family, torn apart by pride and its lust for power, reunited by purity and passion

THE ROYAL HOUSE *of* KAREDES

HP12851

Three Rich HUSBANDS

*When a wealthy man takes a wife,
it's not always for love...*

Meet three wealthy Sydney businessmen who've been
the best of friends for ages. None of them believe in
marrying for love. But all this is set to change....

This exciting new trilogy by

Miranda Lee

begins September 2009 with

THE BILLIONAIRE'S BRIDE OF VENGEANCE

Book #2852

Pick up the next installments of this fabulous trilogy:

THE BILLIONAIRE'S BRIDE OF CONVENIENCE

October 2009

THE BILLIONAIRE'S BRIDE OF INNOCENCE

November 2009

HP12852

REQUEST YOUR FREE BOOKS!

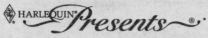

2 FREE NOVELS
PLUS 2
FREE GIFTS!

YES! Please send me 2 FREE Harlequin Presents® novels and my 2 FREE gifts (gifts are worth about $10). After receiving them, if I don't wish to receive any more books, I can return the shipping statement marked "cancel". If I don't cancel, I will receive 6 brand-new novels every month and be billed just $4.05 per book in the U.S. or $4.74 per book in Canada. That's a savings of close to 15% off the cover price! It's quite a bargain! Shipping and handling is just 50¢ per book*. I understand that accepting the 2 free books and gifts places me under no obligation to buy anything. I can always return a shipment and cancel at any time. Even if I never buy another book, the two free books and gifts are mine to keep forever.

106 HDN EYRQ 306 HDN EYR2

Name   (PLEASE PRINT)

Address   Apt. #

City   State/Prov.   Zip/Postal Code

Signature (if under 18, a parent or guardian must sign)

Mail to the **Harlequin Reader Service:**
IN U.S.A.: P.O. Box 1867, Buffalo, NY 14240-1867
IN CANADA: P.O. Box 609, Fort Erie, Ontario L2A 5X3

Not valid to current subscribers of Harlequin Presents books.

Are you a current subscriber of Harlequin Presents books and want to receive the larger-print edition? Call 1-800-873-8635 today!

* Terms and prices subject to change without notice. Prices do not include applicable taxes. Sales tax applicable in N.Y. Canadian residents will be charged applicable provincial taxes and GST. Offer not valid in Quebec. This offer is limited to one order per household. All orders subject to approval. Credit or debit balances in a customer's account(s) may be offset by any other outstanding balance owed by or to the customer. Please allow 4 to 6 weeks for delivery. Offer available while quantities last.

Your Privacy: Harlequin Books is committed to protecting your privacy. Our Privacy Policy is available online at www.eHarlequin.com or upon request from the Reader Service. From time to time we make our lists of customers available to reputable third parties who may have a product or service of interest to you. If you would prefer we not share your name and address, please check here. ☐

HP09R

HARLEQUIN *Presents*

International Billionaires

Life is a game of power and pleasure.
And these men play to win!

THE VIRGIN SECRETARY'S IMPOSSIBLE BOSS
by **Carole Mortimer**

Billionaire Linus loves a challenge.
During one snowbound Scottish night
the temperature rises with his sensible
personal assistant. With sparks flying,
how can Andi resist?

Book #2854

Available September 2009

HP12854

You're invited to join our Tell Harlequin Reader Panel!

By joining our new reader panel you will:

- Receive Harlequin® books—they are FREE and yours to keep with no obligation to purchase anything!
- Participate in fun online surveys
- Exchange opinions and ideas with women just like you
- Have a say in our new book ideas and help us publish the best in women's fiction

In addition, you will have a chance to win great prizes and receive special gifts! See Web site for details. Some conditions apply. Space is limited.

To join, visit us at
www.TellHarlequin.com.

EXTRA

TAKEN: AT THE BOSS'S COMMAND

His every demand will *be met!*

Whether he's a British billionaire, an Argentinian polo player, an Italian tycoon or a Greek magnate, these men demand the very best of everything—and everyone....

Working with him is one thing—marrying him is *quite* another. But when the boss chooses his bride, there's no option but to say I do!

**Catch all the heart-racing stories,
available September 2009:**

The Boss's Inexperienced Secretary #69
by HELEN BROOKS

**Argentinian Playboy,
Unexpected Love-Child #70**
by CHANTELLE SHAW

**The Tuscan Tycoon's
Pregnant Housekeeper #71**
by CHRISTINA HOLLIS

Kept by Her Greek Boss #72
by KATHRYN ROSS

www.eHarlequin.com

HPE0909

I ♥ HARLEQUIN *Presents*

BROUGHT TO YOU BY FANS OF
HARLEQUIN PRESENTS.

We are its editors and authors
and biggest fans—and we'd
love to hear from YOU!

Subscribe today to our online blog at
www.iheartpresents.com